Ryan Fraine turned his head and she met eyes dark as midnight except for a teasing gleam which elicited an expansion of her smile. Lord, she thought as her pupils dilated, but he is attractive!

And he knew it. She read the hint of speculation in his expression correctly. He too liked what he saw. She was not surprised; she had no false modesty and she had known since she was fourteen that her fall of ash-blonde hair and slim, lithe body were attractive to the opposite sex. At one time she had played on it, using her sexual allure to provoke and excite, but that had been a long time ago. She had learned a bitter lesson and for the last few years she had been much more careful.

But it had taken only one interested glance from Ryan Fraine, and she remembered again the breathless, matchless excitement of the game of flirtation, felt once more the tension flick like a whiplash through her nerves and blood, sparkle in her wide eyes and flare along her high cheekbones. This man was dangerous!

SMOKE IN THE WIND

BY

ROBYN DONALD

MILLS & BOON LIMITED
ETON HOUSE   18-24 PARADISE ROAD
RICHMOND   SURREY   TW9 1SR

*First published in Great Britain 1987
by Mills & Boon Limited*

© Robyn Donald 1987

*Australian copyright 1987
Philippine copyright 1987
This edition 1987*

ISBN 0 263 75847 8

*Set in Times Roman 10 on 11 pt.
01-1287-58377 C*

*Printed and bound in Great Britain by
Collins, Glasgow*

For Erin and Sarah and Greg,
who each had more ideas than I
could fit into a single book.

CHAPTER ONE

THE occasion was to be televised, so Venetia Gamble wore one of her good outfits, a dress that made the most of her small slenderness and rendered her hazel eyes as true a gold as the silk. She had managed to persuade her hairdresser to give her a style which, while not as outrageously fashionable as she would have liked, was a little less conventional than the restrained shoulder-length pageboy which went so well with her job as a television reporter. At least she didn't have to worry about making a fool of herself in front of the cameras!

Her lack of height made it difficult to see who else had been invited to the newest and most opulent hotel in Auckland, and pride forbade her to crane her neck, so she contented herself with an interested survey of those people she could see.

'Yes—that's him!' The words came out in a croon of interest from the woman next to her, a slightly overblown actress.

Intrigued, Venetia turned to follow her line of gaze, but could not see beyond a group of men. Without remorse she listened.

'Oh, God, he's gorgeous! Even better in the flesh than in all those news clips and documentaries!'

Her companion, a model so thin that without the extra pounds the camera gave her she looked gaunt, said cheerfully, 'I didn't think you ever watched documentaries, Carol.'

'When Ryan Fraine was in them you couldn't drag me away from the screen, believe me,' Carol Hastings said dramatically. 'I adore men who look as though they don't

7

give a damn about anything! Just look at him! Mean and moody and *sooo* sexy! And an absolutely magnificent lover. In that interview she gave in London Serissa Jordan as much as said so.'

'And got dumped for her pains,' the model said cynically. She caught Venetia's eye and winked, smiling a hello. They knew each other slightly.

Carol Hastings ignored Venetia, fixing her large blue eyes avidly on the man who had been lured out from Britain to set up New Zealand's first private television station. Ryan Fraine's reputation had preceded him. After making his name as a tenacious and nerveless foreign reporter, he had gone independent to produce superb, chilling documentaries, products of a penetrating, diamond-edged intelligence.

They had won him a worldwide reputation, but it was not this which attracted Carol, or any of the women who were reputed to have shared his bed. As well as being tall and elegantly lean, he was superlatively attractive, his angular face hinting at a kind of moody recklessness which made many women wonder hopefully if it were possible to tame him. The more courageous dreamed of releasing the wildness from his truly formidable control and enjoying the onslaught. Venetia respected him for his professionalism and his brilliant, incisive mind, and envied him that effortless, compelling authority.

Ten minutes later she was seated at a table with the preening Carol, an industrialist she recognised from the business pages of the newspaper, and the man who had been the focus of most feminine eyes since he had entered the room.

'Ryan Fraine,' Carol breathed, fluttering eyelashes which had to be false at him. 'And what do you think of New Zealand?'

His dark, saturnine face creased into a smile. 'Three months is not long enough to formulate any opinions worthy of the name.'

'Oh, tactful. Is this the man who is able to describe a whole continent in a brilliant, cynical phrase? Are we too provincial and unsophisticated to cope with the truth?'

As Venetia accepted a menu she decided that the other woman's fluttering lashes and provocative smile weren't going to achieve her aim. It would take more than Carol Hastings and her much vaunted sex appeal to persuade him into an indiscretion. The man wore control like a cloak.

'I like the place very much,' he said now, blandly. 'Not so much the cities, which could be anywhere in the world, but the countryside is spectacular and the life-style enviable.'

A tiny smile escaped Venetia as Carol pouted at this tactful comment. Ryan Fraine turned his head and she met eyes as dark as midnight except for a teasing gleam which elicited an expansion of her smile. Lord, she thought as her pupils dilated, but he is attractive!

And he knew it. She read the hint of speculation in his expression correctly. He too liked what he saw. She was not surprised; she had no false modesty and she had known since she was fourteen that her fall of ash-blonde hair and slim, lithe body were attractive to the opposite sex. At one time she had played on it, using her sexual allure to provoke and excite, but that had been a long time ago. She had learned a bitter lesson, and for the last few years she had been much more careful.

But it had taken only one interested glance from Ryan Fraine, and she remembered again the breathless, matchless excitement of the game of flirtation, felt once more the tension flick like a whiplash through her nerves and blood, sparkle in her wide eyes and flare along her high cheekbones. This man was dangerous!

Carol hadn't missed the little byplay. A note of petulance crept into her voice as she said nastily, 'And are you planning to change channels, Venetia?'

'At the moment I'm very happy with my job.' She slanted a swift smile up at the man next to her and added slyly, 'Of course, I could be persuaded to change my mind.'

'I'm sure you could.' Ryan Fraine sounded totally indifferent, but there was something in the deep voice which made Venetia wish she had not put in that last, teasing comment. 'I wonder what would make you change your mind? More money, or extra prestige?'

The industrialist, a thin, graceful man with a narrow smile, said smoothly, 'In other words, Miss Gamble, are you a materialist or do you want power?'

'Both,' she retorted, smiling. 'You have no idea how seductive the idea of power is when you're a midget! Or how expensive it is to have all your clothes and shoes made specially for you.'

As she had intended, they laughed and the hint of tension dissipated. Venetia relaxed, prepared to enjoy the evening and help others enjoy it too, her slanted golden eyes aglow with expectation. She was not disappointed. The industrialist was pleasantly astringent, Ryan Fraine smoothly urbane, flirting a little with Carol, watching Venetia with lazy, dark eyes which gave very little away.

The occasion was a televised contest to find the best wine waiter in the country and, as guests, the organisers had invited those people who would register with the viewing public. The cameras were busy—often, it seemed, focused on the table where Ryan Fraine sat.

Venetia had no intention of allowing the sudden, febrile excitement which sizzled along her nerves to be displayed through the cameras for public titillation, so she imposed tight control on herself, hiding her emotions beneath heavy lashes. Yet although she rarely looked at the man beside her she felt the weight of his attention, and when the evening was over—the food eaten, the winner applauded—she was not surprised to hear Ryan's voice for her ear only.

'Have you a car here?'

'No,' she said, oddly breathless. 'I'm getting a taxi.'

'I'll take you home.'

She nodded, feeling strangely, absurdly, shy. After all, she was twenty-three, and into those years she had packed more than most women of her age. By now she knew how to deal with almost any situation that came her way, and that included a man obviously interested in her. Since she had left home she had resisted many men, she was quite capable of resisting this one. If she wanted to.

In the car he waited before turning on the engine. 'Do you want to go home yet? We could go on to a night-club...'

She looked at the clock on the dash. Just after eleven. Reluctantly she said, 'Home, please.'

He didn't try to persuade her. Stifling the thought that he probably didn't have to persuade women into anything, she gave him her address.

After they had been on the road for several minutes he asked, 'Do you have an early call?'

'No. But I can't cope with less than eight hours of sleep; my brain refuses to come out of neutral.'

'You're very conscientious. Good at your job, too, but you know that, don't you?'

She was glad that the darkness hid the soft colour in her face. 'I try,' she said lightly. 'A lot of people seem to think that somebody my height must have a dolly little brain to go with the rest of me. It can be very irritating.'

He chuckled. 'Is that why you're so aggressive in your interviews?'

'Partly. I ask the questions I want answered. If that's being aggressive, then I must be. It makes me furious to listen to reporters who let people get away with murder.' She was not defensive; she had been accused of militancy often enough to be able to cope with it. 'You have something of a reputation in that respect, as well. I watched the interview you did with Periera. I could smell his hatred, but it didn't stop you from revealing him for the tyrant he was.'

'He hadn't realised that the programme was going out live. He had two gunmen just out of camera range, but he knew damned well that he didn't dare use them. He made the mistake of thinking he could intimidate me into giving him respectability.'

'Instead, you set into motion the events that toppled him.'

'Hardly. His hold on his little banana republic was pretty precarious. Once his funds were cut off he had nowhere to turn.'

She nodded, remembering with horror the bloody revolution which had rid the little South American country of its vicious ruler. 'It was your interview which showed the rest of the world just what sort of tyrant they were subsidising. Weren't you imprisoned there?'

'Yes, for a few days. I was lucky, I escaped, but thousands died in hellholes like the one I was in. I've seldom met a man more thoroughly evil. He deserved to die.'

His voice was quite indifferent, as though the dictator's death was nothing. Venetia shivered. She had seen the film of that death, the man torn to pieces by the people he had ruled with an iron hand for four years. It had haunted her for weeks; even now she could close her eyes and see the expressions on those gaunt, frenzied faces and the clutching hands which had turned into weapons.

Quickly, to banish the images which were seared into her brain, she said in a muted voice, 'I saw the documentary you made there a couple of years later. It was incredibly good.'

'Thank you. Is this where you live?'

She had been so intent on him that his question came as a surprise. Peering through the windscreen, she saw the profusion of white mountain clematis which almost hid her front door.

'Yes,' she said in a flat little voice because she didn't want the evening to end. She knew she wasn't going to be able to sleep, her blood was beating in slow, heavy tides through her body and she felt at once languorous and wildly excited. 'Would you like a cup of coffee?' she asked tentatively.

For the first time he turned his head. In the dimness of the car the magnificent bone structure of his face was dramatised into an austere beauty of form which dazzled her eyes. There was a flash of white as he smiled and the severity vanished in an uncompromising display of masculine magnetism.

'Why not?' he said blandly.

While she made coffee they discussed a recent juicy political scandal, then her voice faded and she watched breathlessly as he set his cup down and got to his feet, all lean, lithe grace. He didn't say anything as he came towards her, and she made no attempt to move. A foot away he stopped, extending a hand. She looked at the long, spare fingers, then back up to his face. Beneath his lashes there was a sardonic glitter which should have repelled her; she felt that she was standing before a door marked 'Danger'. Unconsciously the tip of her tongue came out to her top lip.

He said nothing. Her heart beat heavily in her ears, she gave a reckless little smile and put her hand in his, allowing him to pull her up against the hard length of his body.

He made no concessions. His mouth was hard and cool and hungry, and later she would realise how carelessly acquisitive that kiss had been, as though he was stamping his brand on her. Light-headed, she swayed, surrendering to the wild attraction which had been building all the evening, and his hands tightened on her yielding flesh, imprisoning her against the fierce tension of his body.

His response was boldly explicit, and she gasped, and then moaned, an erotic little sound deep in her throat as her whole body went up in flames. His head swooped; he buried his face into the arched length of her throat. She could feel the waiting hunger in him as clearly as the heat of his mouth against her skin, and she was suddenly afraid at this firestorm of sensation she had invited.

When his hand slid from her hip to the high curve of her breast she gasped and pushed away, her eyes flaming gold but determined. 'No,' she muttered thickly as she took two difficult steps away from a danger which blazed like a beacon, treacherous yet fascinating.

The hard flush of passion lay along his cheeks, but she could read nothing from his expression. After a moment he said slowly, 'I don't need false modesty to whet my appetites, Venetia.'

She bit her lip, but refused to back down. 'Sorry, but I don't go in for one-night stands. And if that's not your intention you're going too fast.'

He watched her as if she was something strange to him. According to the grapevine he enjoyed sophisticated women. Well, no one could call her naïve, but she had standards. And a strong instinct of self-preservation. She knew what it was like to lose her self-respect; she had no intention of allowing it to happen again.

So she held his gaze, shaking her head, and after a moment he smiled tightly. 'Very well, then. Goodnight.'

He held out his hand; she gave him hers, and realised her mistake when he pulled her against him, holding her still with a hard arm across her back while the other hand pressed insolently against the base of her spine to emphasise in the most blatant way exactly what he wanted from her.

He held her like that for an insulting few seconds, his narrowed, unreadable eyes fixed on her startled face, then said in a deep, uncompromising voice, 'I refuse to play games.'

Venetia had to fight back a surge of desire so intense that for a moment she almost gave in to its seductive pull. Then he released her, and she was safe.

She watched him leave with blank eyes, before going slowly to bed.

Surprisingly enough she slept, waking to the kind of spring morning which lifted the heart. Serenaded by two courting tuis singing and calling in the melia tree, she drank coffee and dressed, examining her face with care to see if anything of last night's happenings showed there. Apart from a suspicion of a shadow in the clear green-gold depths of her eyes she looked exactly as she always did: pert, attractive, her pugnacious little chin lifted at the world.

So much for Ryan Fraine. He was, she decided, far too much for her to deal with. She knew her limitations and that uprush of passion had scared her. It would have been perilously easy to surrender, and she would have woken up that morning despising herself. She would just forget him.

Unfortunately it was not going to be so easy. It began that very day when she was snatching coffee before heading out to an interview.

'Heard you had a very tasty partner at the do last night.' That was Jeff Caldwell, one of the reporters, and with him was the producer's secretary.

Venetia smiled. 'News travels fast.'

'Also,' Jeff said eagerly, 'that you were last seen haring off into the seductive Auckland night with our splendid English hero. What's he like in bed, love?'

'Ask him.'

Too often to be comfortable, Jeff liked to remind her and anyone else who would listen that he had introduced Venetia to the producer, a fact which he considered had got her the job. Even although he had long since given up trying to coax her into bed on the strength of it, he was inclined to adopt a subtly proprietorial attitude towards her.

Now he opened his eyes wide in a parody of astonishment. 'You mean—can it be—am I to understand that you didn't get to first base?'

The secretary grinned and said, 'Don't be an idiot. Would she tell you? Just to satisfy a sordid curiosity, Venetia, is he as good-looking as he photographs?'

'Better,' Venetia told her cheerfully.

Sarah sighed voluptuously. 'Lucky old you! And does he really have that magnificently moody, devilish, damn-you-all attitude to the rest of the world?'

'He does indeed,' Venetia said on a dry note.

Sarah sighed again as Jeff suggested nastily, 'Perhaps you're on the short list to keep his bed warm here.'

Venetia smiled. 'Now, Jeff, you know better than that,' she said, and he looked away, his pale brows drawn petulantly together.

'Well, he can cast those fantastic eyes my way any time he likes,' Sarah said, defusing the rather tense little silence. 'I don't know that I've ever seen another man who projects such a brand of raw, arrogant sexuality, and manages to be intelligent with it.'

Later that day she called Venetia over and showed her a magazine which had an article about him, complete with colour pictures. Venetia simulated a mild interest, but on her way home that night she bought it. The article was fulsome but the photographs were superb; Venetia read it and then hid it in her wardrobe.

There was, however, no escaping him. The evening newspaper had a photograph of them together, she looking smug and he watching her with an amused expression in which the cynicism was only too apparent. Disgusted with herself, she bit her lip and hurled the paper across the room.

But later that evening the item appeared on a television magazine programme.

Venetia was accustomed to possessing that indefinable quality known as presence, but Ryan had more, he had star quality. The camera dwelt lovingly on the planes and angles of his face, yet it was not his saturnine good looks which came over. Put simply, he breathed authority and strength, a fundamental masculine arrogance. Beside him she looked cute and ineffectual.

When it was over she switched the set off and said loudly and defiantly to the empty room, 'It's just sex. That's all. Ignore it. You know how much damage that can do. God knows, you have reason enough to be wary.'

In spite of the wilful, extravagant attraction which had flared to life in the first glance they had exchanged, she knew that she was not going to get tangled up with Ryan Fraine. If he contacted her again she would politely but firmly refuse to see him.

And for the rest of that empty week she kept telling herself that all she had to do was ignore both the man and his effect on her, and eventually both would become unimportant. It shouldn't be difficult. He had only wanted a one-night stand and she was not in the market for that, not for an affair, not even for marriage. Men were nothing but trouble, and Ryan Fraine represented a real threat to the independence she cherished. It was a bitter statement, but one she clung to because her subconscious had been weaving dreams and indulging in softly tinted fantasies.

However, when she woke on Sunday morning to the sound of the telephone and heard his voice, her heart leapt with delight and something treacherously close to relief.

'I've been invited out on a yacht,' he said lightly, without preamble. 'I wondered whether you'd like to come too.'

She had to hide the heady mixture of anticipation and excitement with a cool, restrained voice. 'Thank you, it sounds fun. How big is this yacht?'

'Big enough to take six people in comfort. Why, do you get seasick?'

The teasing note in the question made her flush. She was not going to admit that she was disappointed that there would be other people there. 'No,' she returned a little too cheerfully.

'Good. I'll pick you up in an hour.'

'Shall I prepare lunch?'

He laughed softly. 'No, that's all organised. Just be ready, I don't like being kept waiting.'

As she showered she found herself singing, and frowned, because it had been a long time since she had felt so alive. The magical intensity of anticipation almost frightened her, but she chose not to remember that she had decided not to see him again. After all, with four other people there she had to be perfectly safe!

She chose cotton slacks and a matching top in pale lilac, pulling them on over a brief purple bikini. When his car drew up outside she was ready, a soft flush lighting up her small face.

He was tall and lean and devastating in shorts and a casual shirt. At the sight of him Venetia's pulse threatened to deafen her. In that moment she understood that she was in far deeper than she had realised; he was a challenge she was not equipped to handle.

'Tell me about this yacht,' she said, striving desperately for her usual poise as the car pulled away from the kerb.

'It's called *Hawk*, and it belongs to Logan Sutherland and his wife Fiona.'

'The name sounds familiar.'

He said drily, 'He's on the Producer Board and various other agricultural and pastoral organisations.'

She nodded. 'I've met him. Tall, dark,——'

'Handsome?' he asked with awful irony.

Venetia chuckled. 'Yes, in an intelligent way. He has the most beautiful eyes, and a real pirate's smile. And when he looks at his wife you can feel the flames.'

'You know them that well?'

He didn't have to sound surprised, she thought defiantly. Aloud she explained, 'No, but once at a press conference he gave I happened to be in the corridor afterwards when his wife came up to him. He has a poker face, but for a moment there he looked as if he'd seen heaven.'

'She's a lovely thing,' he said.

A note of cool mockery in his voice rasped across Venetia's nerves, leaving her with the feeling that she had been embarrassingly effusive. Ignoring it, she chatted pleasantly until they reached Westhaven where the yacht was moored. She recognised the Sutherlands; she also recognised the other man there and for a hideous moment she felt the jetty tilt and slide beneath her feet as Fiona Sutherland made the introductions.

'Venetia and I have met,' Brett March said smoothly, his handsome face empty of expression.

Venetia waited, her emotions raw, but he said no more and the breath hissed through her lips in a little gasp of relief. Although the skin on the back of her neck prickled, when she tilted her face towards Ryan he was smiling and she could not see behind the thick screen of his lashes.

The other woman, Brett's partner, was as stunning a redhead as Fiona; her name was Bobby Taylor and she made it quite clear that her sole object was to please Brett.

The day could have been a disaster but, as it wore on, Venetia found that she was enjoying herself. The Sutherlands were charming and intelligent, Brett witty and urbane; even Bobby relaxed when she realised that, far from trying to attract Brett's attention, Venetia did her best to avoid him. Ryan seemed to be enjoying himself too, if his relaxed attitude was any indication.

And the weather was superb, the breeze brisk enough to keep the boat flying through the brilliant waters of the gulf, the sun already showing indications of summer's strength. Some hundreds of Auckland's enormous fleet of pleasure vessels dipped and swayed like multi-coloured birds against a background of islands and peninsulas and long, white beaches.

Venetia made a voluptuous little wriggling movement, her face lifted to the sun with a worshipper's idolatry. Beside her on the deck Ryan slanted a brief appraisal at her vivid little face with its firm jaw and wide, sensuous mouth. She shivered, because his sculptured features were set in cold and forbidding lines. But almost as soon as her eyes widened he smiled and the charm blazed forth again, and she wondered whether she had been mistaken.

She was uneasy after that, watching him surreptitiously while Logan initiated him into the mysteries of sailing, feeling a strange, heated pride because he was quick and clever, as if he already knew a lot about it instead of being totally without experience.

In a way it was a magical day, the sun like a blessing over an enchanted sea, the islands and bays and hills of the gulf mingled in a pattern that was clear and calm and heart-catchingly lovely. Venetia should have been having a wonderful time. But Brett's presence spoiled it for her, although after that initial moment of coolness he gave no hint that each time they had met he had offered her money, first not to marry his cousin, and then, to divorce him.

The interviews were burned into the cells of her brain, her shame and outraged pride, his cool, degrading supposition that she could be bought off. A long time ago, she thought wryly. And such a lot of water under the bridge. In the light of subsequent events she should have taken the money the first time and fled.

'OK, I'd better take the wheel.' Logan's voice broke into her sombre thoughts. 'The entrance into the bay is a bit tricky. You should get yourself a yacht, you know, you're a natural.'

Ryan made a laughing rejoinder and came back to where Venetia sat, slender golden legs dangling over the side.

'Did you enjoy that?' she asked.

'Very much. Do you sail?'

'No, I don't know anything about it. Strictly deck cargo, that's me.'

He smiled and drawled, 'Very attractive deck cargo. You are just what every photographer wants when he tries to conjure up images of summer and the good life.'

'I hope that was a compliment.'

It hadn't sounded like one. There was more than a hint of sarcasm in the words, and the slow appreciation of his dark eyes was almost insulting.

'Oh, I think so,' he said now, as bland as cream. 'Don't all women like to be complimented on their looks?'

'I could lie and say no,' she retorted crisply, fighting the heat that was building in her veins, 'but we're working on it.'

'A feminist, Venetia?'

She returned his mocking smile with interest, enjoying the adrenalin as it pumped into her bloodstream. 'Of course.'

'No time for marriage and children, the love of a good man, all that jazz?'

'No!' she said, the word almost explosive because she was striving to hold her voice steady. Suddenly pale, she looked away. Little rainbows burned on the tips of her lashes; he would see the dampness there so she did the only thing possible, stared straight into the sun until she sneezed.

The subsequent mopping up removed all trace of those tell-tale tears. But because she was afraid of the scrutiny of his dark eyes she said crisply, 'No woman nowadays has to give up all that makes her life interesting and worthwhile to dwindle into a wife and mother. If you work things out carefully, you can have it all. I don't intend making sacrifices—in fact, I don't think anyone is ever thanked for sacrificing themselves, not for a husband, not for children. Gratitude, if you're lucky enough to get it, is no substitute for fulfilment.'

'So you're a modern, liberated woman?'

'Very much so.' Regaining control of her expression, she looked back at him. Something daunting in the saturnine features made her ask, 'Don't you like the species?'

'Not a lot.' He leaned back against the stanchion, settling wide shoulders into a comfortable position. 'I am, of course, prejudiced. My mother was before her time. Although my father worked himself into the grave to make money, she bought an antique shop because she hated to stay at home. As a small child I wanted only one thing: a mother who was a mother, not a tired visitor at both ends of the day.'

'Perhaps she wouldn't have been so tired if someone had helped her in the house,' Venetia suggested.

'She had household help. I was never neglected, not physically. However, I understood at a very early age that I came a poor second to her business.'

'It doesn't sound as though she should have had children.'

He smiled cynically. 'She had me because at the age of thirty she felt the need to obey her biological imperative. She was quite satisfied with her life; I was the one to suffer.'

'Most children feel that their parents fail them in some ways.' It was difficult to be objective because Venetia's heart was wrung at the thought of the little boy who, with the innocent selfishness of childhood, wanted to be the centre of his mother's world rather than a small figure hovering on the periphery.

He shrugged, his dark eyes shrewd as they rested on her face. 'So they do. Tell me, what do you think most children would prefer? A mother who can be relied on to be there, or a succession of pleasant but basically uninterested childminders?'

'That's not the only alternative,' she protested.

'No? A daycare centre? That simply means more children to a minder, even less attention.'

She retorted rashly, 'Do children need such undiluted attention? Do you think women should devote themselves solely to their husbands and children?'

'Me?' He lifted mocking brows. 'I don't supply answers, Venetia, I pinpoint the questions. But I feel quite strongly that any woman who wants a child should be prepared to devote herself to that child at least until it goes to school. Children need stability.'

'I notice that you don't mention the father,' she said acidly. 'Doesn't he bear some responsibility for both creating that life and caring for it?'

'Of course, and if the mother and father can come to some sort of arrangement for sharing the responsibility as well as the work, so much the better. Unfortunately, the world is not organised that way.'

'Because most men are too chauvinistic to accept that sort of situation,' she retorted sweetly.

He grinned, wickedly mocking. 'That's woman's fault too—she should bring up her sons to be as liberated as her daughters.'

She laughed, glad that the intensity of the last few minutes had been transmuted into humour. 'You want it all ways!'

'You must admit that life for most women was probably easier in the days when they expected to stay at home with the children.'

Venetia wasn't going to let him get away with that. 'Easier, possibly, but much less challenging.'

'And a challenge is important to you, isn't it? I was talking to Jeff Caldwell yesterday, and he regaled me with some of your more outrageous exploits.'

Surprised, and feeling ridiculously guilty, as though she had been showing off, she said, 'Oh, you don't want to believe everything Jeff says. In a funny way he feels responsible for me.'

'Perhaps because he got you your position?'

She jerked upright, her eyes sparkling, molten gold. 'Did he tell you that? He introduced me to Stan Carpenter, but Stan is a professional, there's no way that he'd employ anyone unless he was satisfied they could do the work.'

Her indignation amused him. 'You don't have to convince me. I agree, you're very good at your job.'

She said bluntly, 'It's important to me that I'm good. People tend to underrate me because they think I'm little and pretty and cute...'

She stopped, staring at him in gathering anger as he threw his head back and laughed. After a moment he said drily, 'Little you certainly are, and pretty, but you're about as cute as a tiger cub. You look like Tinkerbell and you come on like the crocodile, all claws and teeth, Venetia, and a will as strong as steel.'

'How do you know that?'

He smiled, leaned forward and brushed her mouth with his own, lightly, lazily, almost casually, yet when he lifted his head her heart was thumping in a frenzy and she felt sweat break out at her temples.

'Because,' he told her calmly, 'you respond like a tigress to a man, yet you can cut off without too much difficulty when things get too heavy.'

Without difficulty! She had to be the best actress in the world if she had convinced him that her refusal to go to bed with him had been made easily. She almost laughed, but her sense of self-preservation kept her silent. It was not sensible to let him know just how close to surrender she had been.

'Well, I've been called worse things,' she murmured sweetly. 'I rather like tiger cubs. And crocodiles do at least smile! Once I had to ride a camel; now, that's a nasty, evil-tempered, strong-willed creature, if you like!'

She made him laugh with her description of the occasion and listened with pleasure as he capped it with a vivid and hilarious recital of the pitfalls of dealing with a llama which had a violent and determined temperament. By the time he had finished the boat was at anchor in a tiny bay and Logan was organising the dinghy to take them ashore.

CHAPTER TWO

THE bay was no more than a cove overhung by pohutu-kawa trees, the little crescent of white sand cut off abruptly by cliffs with rocky outliers where waves crawled like tame tigers. In a storm it would be a magnificent sight of spume and chaos, but today it was like a small piece of heaven. Sheep grazed on the hills, lambs called and played and frolicked in their typecast innocence, and seagulls wheeled overhead, diving down as soon as their greedy eyes discerned the picnic lunch.

Fiona had packed delicious brown rolls and an assort-ment of salads, including a delectable chicken and avo-cado, along with a game pie and cold meats for those who preferred them. To follow there was fruit, globes of tan-geloes as vividly coloured as goldfish, green island paw-paws, the last of the year's pears, a little wizened but still juicy and superbly full of flavour. For those who had used up all their appetite there were tiny mandarins, sweet and easily peeled; ideal morsels to finish the meal.

'I've brought coffee in thermoses,' Fiona said when they were all finished, 'but how would you like billy tea?'

She seemed to be looking at Venetia, who answered promptly, 'I've never had it, but I'll try anything once.'

Fiona grinned. 'You a New Zealander, and you've never drunk billy tea? Shame on you!'

'Just because your father was an addict, and you drank it with your mother's milk, you like to feel superior,' Logan teased her. 'Come on, men, billy tea is the pre-serve of males. We gather the wood and get the fire going, and we make it. Women always lose courage at the last moment and hold back on the tealeaves. It's not the

26

genuine stuff unless it comes spitting and snarling out of the mug.'

There was plenty of driftwood about, enough for a dozen large bonfires. As Venetia helped Fiona pack up the remnants of their lunch she kept a watch on Ryan, and was astonished to see that it was he who set the fire.

'Clearly he knows what he's doing,' Fiona commented, following her gaze. 'At first sight you'd think he was too sophisticated for this sort of thing, wouldn't you? But there's no mistaking that air of competence. It gives him away.'

Her eyes travelled from Ryan's lean, athletic frame to that of her husband, who also possessed that aura, and from him to Brett, who certainly didn't. Fiona and Venetia wore identical small, satisfied smiles as their eyes met, but neither said anything for Bobby was too close, sitting disconsolately on the edge of the rug, her slender, boneless body displayed to best advantage. She looked forlorn, as though she only felt alive when watched by someone else, preferably an admiring male.

'Let's go down,' Fiona said, and immediately Bobby set off for the beach. Fiona's laughing, sympathetic gaze followed her; she grinned at Venetia and began to tell her about her three children who were spending the day with their grandmother.

When they got the tea it was hot and smoky and strong, but it was pleasant, not the vicious brew Venetia had been expecting.

'I can see why it's a tradition. It's delicious,' she said, lifting her eyes to laugh into Logan's. Turning to Ryan who stood a little behind her, she asked, 'Do you like it?'

Some emotion in the depths of his eyes was quickly suppressed. He said drily, 'Compared to some of the brews I've drunk this is nectar.'

Venetia chuckled, a warm, sensuous little sound. For a second it seemed as though they were all held motionless there in the warmth of the spring sun, a group of

beautiful people, as artificial and frozen in time as a
painting by Watteau.

Then a gull screamed and as if it had been a signal they
moved, and Venetia became aware of Brett's glance on
her. Angry at the contempt she saw there, she stared defiantly at him, refusing to back down until another in-
sistent stare impinged, dragging her attention sideways to
Ryan's uncompromising features.

He recognised the other man's scorn. The dark gaze
flicked from face to face, lingering impassively on hers.
As if Brett did not exist she met Ryan's eyes steadily, her
little chin tilted at an angle. When Brett was drawn away
by the watchful Bobby she didn't even notice.

Ryan lifted his mug of tea and drank, never taking his
eyes from her, and she was suffused with a pang of desire so intense that she felt it break out as a wave of sensation. Her skin tightened and prickled.

'Cold?' he murmured, just for her, his tone making it
more than obvious that he knew she wasn't.

Well, two could play at that. She let her eyes wander
over the breadth of his shoulders and chest, then said
demurely, 'Oh no, I think a goose walked over my grave.'

Laughter and a knowing, sensual appreciation gleamed
beneath his lashes. His eyes dropped to her mouth as he
mocked, 'What an inconvenient—goose.'

Venetia drew a ragged breath. She had felt desire before, but she had never known this fury of passion which
overrode all of the tenets of safe, civilised behaviour. She
wanted him so much that she could almost feel his
strength and the primitive hunger of his taking; dimly she
heard the conversation of the others, but all she understood was the explicit, frank message in Ryan's deep
gaze.

It was frightening, and thrilling, and her response was
every bit as blatant as his desire.

Then Fiona tossed a laughing remark their way and the
stark hunger that looked out from his eyes disappeared,

banished by a strength of will Venetia could only respect. He was smiling as he turned to answer, leaving her almost shaking with the force of her emotions.

Nothing had ever been like this before. Nothing. It hurt to look at him, because he was so beautiful, so splendidly proportioned that her body yearned for him. She had always jeered at the idea of love at first sight; even now, the cool, analytical part of her brain accepted that she was suffering from an overwhelming physical attraction. Yet with the excitement, the breathless passion, there was an intense curiosity to know him, a desire to understand him, a hunger that went far beyond the sensual.

Venetia had never run from anything in her life. Her childhood had been marked by a long series of escapades which had terrified the aunt who had adopted her when her parents were killed, and made her cousin Elizabeth shudder with fear. Even the painful episode of her short marriage had not doused her hunger for life, although it had made her much more cautious about the emotional aspects: she had never allowed another man to become her lover.

That single disastrous experience of desire had burned her so severely that she never wanted to expose herself to it again. And somehow she knew that what she had suffered with Sean was nothing to the way Ryan could make her suffer, if she were stupid enough to let him get close to her.

Uncharacteristically subdued, she spent much of the pleasant, lazy afternoon watching him from beneath her lashes, telling herself that she was a fool. Then he would smile at her and each time she drowned in that suffocating sensuality, her wide eyes vulnerable for a fleeting second.

They set off towards Auckland at about four o'clock, the yacht one of an enormous homecoming fleet, and sailed serenely past more exquisite islands towards a city

of golden haze. A wind came up, cool and testing, and
Venetia shivered. It was like the let-down at the end of an
absorbing fantasy novel, when you realise that there are
no elf-kings or dragons, no jewelled cities and talking
beasts, just the grey workaday world.

'Why don't you go below?' Ryan said. When she
shook her head he looped his arms about her, pulling her
into the warmth of his body. This time her shiver had
nothing to do with the wind, and everything to do with
the fact that they were both wearing shorts, and his legs
against hers engendered sensations which were erotic and
extremely disturbing.

'I'm not really cold,' she said quickly, trying to turn
away. He let her swivel until she was facing away from
him then tightened the cage of his arms, cuddling her into
the hard security of his body. She finished lightly, 'Be-
sides, it must be just as cold there.'

His chuckle was lazily mocking, but he let her go when
Fiona came past them to go below and wash up the cups
in the efficient little galley.

It was a relief to dry them for her, and after that
Venetia admired the luxurious fittings of the rest of the
yacht, and by then they were back at the marina. She
helped as much as she could in the berthing of the yacht,
mainly by keeping out of the way, watching with interest
as Logan and Fiona, aided by Ryan and to a lesser ex-
tent Brett, made everything tidy. Back on the jetty she
nodded and agreed that yes, they must meet again,
knowing and regretting the fact that they probably
wouldn't.

In the car she flicked an enquiring glance at his profile. Her eyes settled, tracing the forceful lines of nose
and chin and brow, then were withdrawn and until they
arrived home she stared unseeing through the windscreen.

As she put the key into her lock he said, 'I'm sorry I
annoyed you that night.'

She turned a surprised face to his unreadable one. He was smiling, yet she had the uneasy feeling that it was not an indication of his feelings.

'My less than gracious reaction to your refusal,' he supplied smoothly. 'I'm not usually so churlish.'

She was glad to make a small production out of unlocking the door because it hid the fleeting colour along her cheekbones. 'That's all right.'

Heavens, but the words sounded stilted!

'Am I forgiven?'

She pushed the door open and said airily, 'Yes, of course you are.'

She didn't invite him in and he left without touching her or making any plans for another meeting. As she shut the door behind him Venetia frowned and bit her bottom lip.

A long shower helped a little, but more reviving was the cup of coffee she drank before the window while the sun sank over the houses opposite, warming the lazy air with gold. For no reason she was chilled.

That Sunday marked the beginning of a strange interlude in her life. She knew that she should not go out with him, but she did, and didn't know whether to be pleased or frustrated that he never touched her. Pleased, she suspected, because as long as he kept his distance she could go on fooling herself that she was quite safe with him. He took her to dinner and to a season of foreign films; they discovered that they had similar likes and dislikes and shared a keen sense of the ridiculous which kept both of them immensely entertained through a long, outrageously pretentious art film. Afterwards, while drinking wine and exchanging opinions with two incredibly earnest men who vied with each other in producing orotund and meaningless comments, it was all Venetia could do to keep a still face. She didn't dare meet Ryan's wicked eyes, and in the car on the way home his brilliant imitation of them made her laugh so much that she got a stitch and had to clutch her sore side while she begged him to stop.

He laughed but did so, to say a few silent minutes later, 'One of these days I'll make a film that's both popular and a critical success.'

Startled, because it was the first time he had ever let her past the sophisticated mask he wore, she asked cautiously, 'Another documentary?'

'No.'

He clearly meant to close the subject, but Venetia was not a reporter for nothing. Snuggling down into the seat she said casually, 'Why did you give up making documentaries? You were absolutely brilliant.'

He waited so long that she thought he was going to refuse to answer. Finally he said sombrely, 'I burnt out. Watching people and countries bleed to death exhausts the spirit.'

She nodded, knowing the sort of burn-out he was referring to. Most reporters developed a thick skin, a cynical attitude which helped shield them from constant exposure to the very worst that humanity could do. His admission reassured her that Ryan was more than the hard sophisticate he seemed to be; he had areas of vulnerability.

'So you came out here, to political infighting and backstabbing. Nice and clean.'

She expected him to laugh, but his voice was heavy as he returned, 'Compared to some of the situations I've been in, this is paradise. You people have a basic kindness and compassion which the rest of the world seems to have forgotten. Oh, you have the faults of your size and your position; you're insular and you can be smug, but in the main you do really care about each other. It's a refreshing change, believe me.'

'Is that why you came here, down to the bottom of the world?'

He laughed, but answered readily enough. 'Setting up the station is a challenge. I've always been addicted to challenges.'

Was that how he saw her? As a challenge to be overcome?

Back at home, when he had driven away, she sat down on the side of her bed and admitted that she was almost in love with him. She was, she thought moodily, in deep, deep trouble, and convincing herself that the best thing to do was never to see Ryan Fraine again was going to be the most difficult task she had ever set herself. And perhaps the most necessary.

His previous liaisons had been with sophisticated, knowledgeable women like the actress Serissa Jordan. He assumed that Venetia was the same sort of woman: assured, modern, able to hold her own in the tough world she had chosen to work in.

In a way he was quite right. She had always been independent, prided herself on it, been thankful for it, but she was beginning to wonder if her vaunted self-reliance had been unbreached simply because she had never met a man powerful enough to get behind the walls. The Venetia behind those glossy barricades was appallingly open to the sort of forbidden temptation that was Ryan Fraine.

If she continued to accept his invitations she would have no excuse for not surrendering to his ultimate intention. Bed, she thought defiantly, repressing a hidden feminine shiver of anticipation at the mental picture of his lean, strong body poised above hers, blocking out the world. The image of strength and weakness stayed in her mind; she could see her small slenderness open to invasion by his vital male force . . .

'Oh, God,' she whispered, shaken by the sensual imagery. Her mouth was dry; she had to moisten it with coffee before she could say loudly and firmly, 'OK, so the man's desirable. So, remember, was Sean. You couldn't curb your sexual urges then, and look where that got you! Pregnant and married at eighteen! A disaster.'

The words were flat and heavy. Even thinking about that period in her life made her shudder. She had given in to barely understood desires, and then, ashamed and frightened, to the insistence of her aunt and uncle that she marry Sean March to give the child she carried a name. And then she had lost the baby, and suffered a dreadful couple of months with a trapped, resentful boy of a husband until his cousin, Brett March, had insultingly and contemptuously once more offered her money to leave him.

Furiously bitter at his assumption that she had planned the whole thing because the March family was rich and socially prominent, she had taken it, using it to support herself while she put herself through a journalism course. But that brief capitulation to the urges of her body had done far more harm than just shaming her.

Unable to bear the gossip in the small town which had been their home all their lives, her aunt and uncle had left with their younger daugher and come to Auckland. Because, as her Aunt Janice had said, 'I don't want the boys here to think that Elizabeth is—well, easy.'

Like you...

The unspoken words had slashed at Venetia. She had replied woodenly, 'No one who knew Elizabeth would think that.'

'Oh, a reputation is lost far easier than it's gained. Anyway, your uncle found this job. It's not quite as good as the one he had at home, but at least...'

Her aunt had a habit of letting her sentences trail away to nothingness, but only when she had made the meaning quite plain.

From then on Venetia had not lived with her aunt and uncle. Instead, fiercely determined to control her life, she had made a career and built a carefully constructed existence around her decision never to compromise her independence again. No man had ever been allowed emotional or physical closeness; she had had no romances, no lovers.

She had channelled her naturally adventurous spirit into a cool assertiveness, refusing to allow anyone the right to make decisions for her. It had worked very well.

Until Ryan Fraine.

He was the wild card, the one who could destroy her serene, safe life. If she allowed him to get to her she was not going to be able to accept a passionate affair with a cheerful farewell at the end of it. Something dark and disturbing about the man called to hidden needs and hungers in her, hitherto unknown, unrealised. He attracted her on too many levels.

There was that blazing sensuality, the virile masculine grace which drew all feminine eyes. Then there was the fact that he was an excellent companion, he made her think, he kept her interested. They even shared the same sense of humour. But there was an even more potent factor in his fascination, one she did not really understand, except that she felt it in the core of her soul.

At some basic, completely primitive level, she recognised him.

Venetia had never been in love, not even with the boy she had married. She realised now that what she had been convinced was love was nothing more than an overwhelming physical attraction, and perhaps her yearning to be loved, not because it was a duty but for herself alone. The emotion that impelled men and women towards marriage or folly was unknown to her. And the results of her first experience of desire had given her a great mistrust of it.

Marriage as an institution she respected. Some lucky couples found friendship and affection after the first violent transports of desire were sated. Her mind went back to Fiona and Logan Sutherland. There was no mistaking the strength of the feelings between them. That sort of marriage lasted because it was based on far firmer foundations than evanescent lust. If Venetia ever married she was determined it would be to a man who saw more than the pretty face and curvy little body which came over so well on the television screen.

And that was possibly why Ryan was such a danger. Oh, he made it quite clear that he was all male, he liked her physical attributes, but he enjoyed the quick thrust and parry of her conversation, and he was really interested, perhaps too interested, in the way her brain worked. She suspected that she could become addicted to that clever, incisive wit and the brilliant analytical skills which made his conversation so fascinating.

So... if she valued her freedom she had to say goodbye to him before he became necessary to her. He was not a man to whom women would ever be a necessity except physically. His hard-edged self-sufficiency was completely uncompromising.

Standing in the warm, bright bedroom she shivered, and determined, quite coolly, that that was it, she wasn't going to see him again.

It might have worked. She was strong-willed, made cautious by instincts as old as time. But will-power went for nothing because she was captured by something even more fundamental than caution. The attraction between the sexes is capable of making even the most wary person reckless.

And at a public relations exercise—all media people and rather good wine—they met Brett March again, this time with a blonde whose dimples belied her flat shark's eyes. He looked Venetia over with the calm insolence she found so offensive, but he was polite, even saying as their conversation wound down, 'By the way, Sean sends you his regards.' His amused eyes slid across to Ryan's face. He explained pleasantly, 'Sean is Venetia's husband.'

If he had expected an interesting reaction he was disappointed, for nothing showed in the sardonic mask of

Ryan's face and Venetia said dispassionately, 'Was, Brett. We divorced, remember?'

'After one of the shortest marriages in history,' he murmured, apparently not at all put out. 'I'll give him your love, shall I?'

'Do that.' She even produced a smile, rather proud of her insouciance.

On the way home she wondered whether to tell Ryan anything about that doomed marriage; she hated raking it up and would have preferred to say nothing, but it was his total lack of reference to it which persuaded her to confide in him.

A little tentatively she said, 'I was married at eighteen.'

His mouth tightened. 'You started young.'

She asked curtly, 'How old were you when you lost your virginity?'

He shrugged, and that disconcerting thread of scorn disappeared from his voice. '*Touché.* About the same age. You don't have to tell me about it, you know. It's no business of mine.'

'I didn't like Brett March's insinuations. Sean is his cousin, and as Brett never does anything without expecting profit from it he can't see that I didn't marry Sean because he is one of the rich Marches. Old money, you know.' She mimicked an affected drawl.

'Why did you marry him?'

She gave a little sad choke of laughter. 'Oh God, because my family insisted. I was pregnant, you see.'

'I see.' His voice was toneless. 'So what happened to the child?'

'I miscarried at six months. It was a little girl and she died.'

So much pain glossed over in a flat little statement.

'So that was the end of the marriage?'

She nodded. 'Sean was a year older than me, only a boy. Both of us were resentful at being forced into marriage.'

'Possibly your parents were thinking of the child's welfare.'

'My aunt and uncle. My parents died when I was a baby, and my father's brother and his wife brought me up. Yes, they were thinking of the child——' but more of their reputation, '—we were all thinking of the child. When she died there was nothing left.'

She hated the glib, unemotional words, but that was the only way she could speak of her baby without crying. As it was, her voice trembled on the last word; she had to bite her lip to stop the tears.

She felt his searching glance and was comforted by the swift clasp he gave her tense hands as they lay in her lap.

'Poor little one,' he said on a rare note of compassion. 'Would you have told me anything about it if March hadn't tried to make trouble?'

'No.'

The car slowed outside her flat, and stopped. Ryan switched the engine off and turned to look at her; she was biting her lip again and in the light of the street lamp he could see the sheen of tears in her eyes, masked though they were by her lashes. She turned an astonished face towards him as he unclipped both seat-belts and pushed his seat back, reaching out for her.

He pulled her into his lap and held her gently, his mouth tender on her forehead, enclosing her in a cocoon of warmth and protection. Weakly, because she sensed that this was far more dangerous to her than his blazing sensuality, she relaxed, turning her face obediently as his mouth searched out the smooth half-moons of her eyelids, the high sweep of cheekbones, the frail vulnerability of her temples. He smelt of man, exciting and comforting and subtly sexual, but his mouth made no overt demands on her and she sank deeper into the spell of his protective strength.

Just when his tactics changed she was never able to pinpoint, nor did she know whether the change was deliberate or not. But gradually the kisses became deeper and more demanding, and the pleasant haze of pleasure about her became shot with the brilliant hues of desire. She gasped, and he moved into her mouth with a sudden half-angry thrust, taking possession of its sweet depths.

Passion fountained through her body; she felt her hands clutch at his shoulders and when his mouth moved down her throat she tipped her head back to allow him access to its gleaming length.

Against her skin he murmured, 'Let's go inside, Venetia.'

Once inside, all of her inhibitions, all of the wariness, faded away. Waiting while he locked the door she felt her bones liquefy with intense desire. But when he turned to her she asked in a tight little voice, 'Would you like some coffee?'

Ryan smiled. 'No. Come here.'

He watched as she came towards him, the smile not softening in the least the hard, exciting line of his mouth. Venetia felt a little spark of defiance at that arrogant, imperious smile. She wanted to see desire written as large in his face as she suspected it was in hers; she stopped a little way in front of him and lifted her chin a fraction, saying nothing.

His eyes narrowed. 'Playing games, Venetia?'

'Just making a point,' she said striving for coolness.

He laughed deep in his throat and reached out and brought her to him with implacable hands. Softly, as his mouth came down towards hers he said, 'Point taken. Now, stop trying to score off me and think only of this...'

It was impossible to think of anything else. At the touch of his mouth, hard and uncompromising and demanding, her head whirled and the world with it, snipping away all the excellent reasons why this should not be happening. For a second she stood motionless and rigid, her mouth as tightly closed as her eyes, and then she moaned, a funny, terrified little sound from deep in her throat, and opened herself to the thrust of his kiss, surrendering to the force of a passion beyond anything she had ever experienced with Sean all those years ago. That had been the hot blood of youth; this, she thought despairingly, was a force as elemental and unforgiving as nature, as rapturous, as impossible to resist. Only this man, only Ryan...

With an expertise she found intimidating he made himself master of her responses, drawing from her a desperate reaction she could not control because she was lost in sensual enchantment. His kiss was magic, the scent of him an aphrodisiac of uncanny strength. She shuddered, her small face lifted raptly as he buried his mouth in the warm arc of her throat. Heat coursed through her body; passion was a series of shivering progressions which overwhelmed her at last so that she found herself mindlessly whispering his name in a cracked little voice.

'You feel like flames,' he whispered. 'Hot and fierce... I'm going to burn myself, yet I don't care...' His tongue stabbed swiftly into the delicate whorls of her ear.

She flinched at the erotic charge, aware from the rapid thunder of his heart that he was captured by the same primitive mystery as she. Sighing, she slid her small hands beneath his shirt, worked them up the wide expanse of his back. Beneath those questing fingers his skin was like oiled silk, supple and warm over the shifting movements of his muscles. Venetia throbbed with the primeval call of female to male, her subtle, alluring response to his lovemaking filling the golden, gleaming wells of her eyes beneath lids heavy with promises.

'Ah, you feel so good,' she whispered and pulled herself further into him, pressing against his lean body in an invitation as explicit as it was irresistible.

He said something that should have shocked her, a dark, forthright expresson of what she was doing to him, then picked her up and carried her into her bedroom. For an instant she lay rigid in his arms, for the first time facing directly the fact that now there was no turning back. This was what she had always feared, this overwhelming flood of sensation. This was why, after that bitter mockery of an adolescent marriage, she had held back, refusing to allow any man to go beyond a few kisses.

Her aunt's strictures had frightened her, making her see herself as a woman unable to control her desires; now she realised that it was only because she had known in the innermost, most hidden parts of her soul that one day she would meet a man who would touch her so strongly that she would be helpless with love for him.

He set her on her feet, his hands on her shoulders, his thumbs pushing her chin up to his merciless scrutiny. Fearlessly, her eyes smouldering with the realisation of her newly discovered love, she looked back at him, asking no quarter.

A smile twisted his mouth. 'So small,' he said quietly, 'like a little lion cub, fiercely brave, open and valiant, with a screwball courage which scares the hell out of me. Do you want me to go, Venetia?'

He would take nothing she wasn't prepared to give freely. The dark flush of passion lay along those bold cheekbones, yet he had the strength to leave her if she said no. Had he ever been loved? Oh, from his mother on there had been women who admired him for his actions, for that effortless authority and the hard masculine strength, but had any woman ever seen beyond it to the child who had thought himself rejected?

The thoughts swirled through the heated recesses of her mind. She could give him that, the rare and precious gift of love, selflessly and without counting the cost. Anticipating a refusal, he began to smile, a slow, unpleasant movement of his lips, and she said huskily, 'No, I don't want you to go, Ryan.'

He hesitated, his expression guarded, then commanded, 'Undress for me,' and sat down on the edge of the bed.

Was it a test? The room was dark, lit only by a lamp outside in the hall, and that darkness gave her the confidence to slide the tab of her zip down and pull the swathe of her dress over her head. Beneath it she wore only french knickers; she stood shyly watching his impassive face, unaware that the light through the doorway gilded her outline in soft radiance, tenderly highlighting the soft curves of her breasts, the narrow indentation of her waist.

Embarrassed by his smouldering gaze, she half turned away, stripping off the satin garment, her movements displaying the supple curve of her spine and the dimples on either side.

'You are perfect,' Ryan said huskily. 'A perfect miniature.'

He touched her as though she were a rare and fragile thing, but after a few seconds the gentle, almost tentative movements became transmuted; he revealed his desire through subtly experienced caresses which traced the soft curves of her body. Venetia thought dizzily that until that moment she had been only half aware, half awake.

His mouth was warm and seeking as it roved from her throat to the vulnerable hollows in her shoulders. She shivered at the slight roughness of his tongue, the faint dampness where he tasted her.

Her skin tightened and he said on a half-breath, 'You're cold,' and put her between the sheets, shedding his clothes with economical movements which didn't hide his impatience. As he came down beside her faint memories of the past made Venetia brace herself, but it seemed that in making love, as in his work, he was a perfectionist.

Those merciless, maddening hands found her secret places, revealed to her the hidden fountains of eroticism in her body, so that before long she was whimpering in frustration, her hands frantic on his body as she tried to kindle in him the same explosive sensations he was causing in her.

'Yes,' he said on an impeded, driven note, turning his face into the warm curve of her breasts. 'Oh God, darling, yes, yes, *yes...*'

More than life, more than happiness, Venetia wanted him; the tight, waiting sensations in her stomach and thighs drove her beyond sanity, and he was goading her further into madness with small, soft kisses across her shoulders, girdling her waist, smiling, his ragged breath belying that fierce control.

She winced with need, her body aching for satisfaction, and knew that she was in deep trouble because he was able to control the passion which held him in thrall. He wanted her, he would enjoy her, but for him she was just another desirable woman.

It was her need to force him to share the uncontrollable hunger which ate at her that led her to her next actions. Gathering courage she slid sinuously down the lean, hard length of his body, treating him to a taste of those elusive, tormenting little kisses. Every muscle in his strong body clenched, and for a moment she thought that his basic need to be in control would force him to twist free, but although he shuddered he did not stop her. He lay back on the crisp white sheets and watched with hooded eyes as she explored him, sprawling across him in abandon, glorying in the tension which locked his muscles.

She laughed softly, almost soundlessly, and kissed from his shoulder down his arm, delighting in the contrast between the taut power of his upper arm, the thudding blue veins in his wrist and the lean strength of his fingers. When her small teeth bit into the mound at the base of his thumb she rejoiced at the slow, harsh indrawing drag of his breath into his empty lungs.

'Ah, do you like that?' she breathed, holding his eyes with her mocking glance.

From beneath his heavy eyelids there glittered a promise and a warning, but she was too ardently in love with her work to heed either. All those years ago her only previous experience of sex had been perfunctory and selfish; she had been conscious only of her own body, her own needs. She and Sean had been children, intent as children always are only on their own gratification. Now, with added maturity and the understanding that love gives, she wanted to give Ryan everything that she could without heeding the cost. But even as she discovered how arousing it was to make love to him a rigour of sensation caught her unawares; before she could control it her hips moved in a rhythm as old as time, betraying what was happening to her.

Satisfacton curled the corners of his mouth, but apart from a single harsh breath he made no other response. Once more she moved lightly, smoothly across the beloved territory of his body, scattering kisses as she went, savouring the salty skin beneath its light tangle of hair, the form and shape of him. Her hands shaped and touched, lingered then swept on quickly.

At last she lowered her head to the hard male nipples, and as if he could bear it no longer he groaned. Both the promise and the warning blazed forth from his face and he wrested control from her in the one way that satisfied them both, invading the heated warmth of her body with the primitive intention of stamping himself on to her life. He answered her totally feminine challenge with fierce masculine aggression.

She had anticipated a little pain—it had been so long since she had made love—but her unashamed arousal of

him rebounded on to her so that when he stormed the
citadel of her body she welcomed her conqueror in with
no pangs either physical or mental, just joyous abandon.

He said her name, and the hard, masculine aggression
eased into stillness; she moaned softly, holding herself as
still as he was, adjusting to his weight and the scent and
feel of fully aroused male, preparing herself for even
greater pleasures. It was so far removed from her previous experience that all remembrance of Sean's embraces fled to the furthermost regions of her mind. She
said, 'Ryan,' her voice velvet with all that she was feeling.

It was all the encouragement he needed. He made a
strange little noise deep in his throat, gathered all that
awesome male strength and possessed himself completely of all that she offered so lovingly, and what followed forced her into a world of sheer sensation which
for ever changed her view of herself. Torn from her
throat, an agonised little sound died stillborn before she
met his passion with a totally uninhibited response as
fierce as his, as completely immersed in the moment, as
lost to all the restraints of civilised behaviour.

It was like a madness, fevered and unreal, and it was
the whole world: nothing existed but the agonising quest
for fulfilment. With a wild disbelief and wonder she felt
the first tense, exhilarating sensations begin to build deep
inside her. Her head tossed from side to side on the pillow; she gasped, 'I can't—I don't——'

'Yes,' he said hoarsely and she surrendered, terrified
yet ecstatic, as his body drove into her.

She convulsed and her body exploded with sensation,
thunderbolt piled on top of thunderbolt, faster and ever
faster until at last she cried out and soared over some
unknowable edge, only dimly aware that the same thing
was happening to him, that he too had given a muffled
cry at the moment of savage ecstasy and then had col-

lapsed, all that splendid male pride tamed by exhaustion.

After a long time he moved and she asked sleepily, 'What are you doing?'

'Going home.' The answer was curt and without expression, warning her to hold back the protest which trembled on her tongue. Silently, her heart aching, she watched as he dressed, worshipping his lean, vital strength, the source of such indescribable rapture.

She got up and pulled on her robe, pushing her hair back from her stiff face.

CHAPTER THREE

THE weeks that followed were the happiest of Venetia's life. In Ryan she discovered a man she could trust completely, a man, she realised slowly, whom she loved. It didn't even hurt that he was not in love with her; it was enough that he wanted her. There was plenty of time to show him that they were meant for each other.

First of all, his resentment had to be dealt with. For some reason it was important to him to be in command of every situation, and she had only to look at him in a certain way, her lashes half hiding the gold of her eyes, and he could not prevent his fierce, uncontrollable response. And she rejoiced in the knowledge of her power, her laughter gleeful, her small, passionate body like wildfire and lightning in his arms as he groaned out his desire into the heated satin of her throat. She loved him, and because of that she held back nothing but the words, yet the hunger that had drawn them together was never sated.

But always afterwards he withdrew to a mental stronghold where she could not reach him. He never spent the whole night in her bed, or took her to his. It hurt, but Venetia learned patience, and an optimism which surprised her, and a love which seemed to grow in quantum leaps day by day.

'Oh, but you are beautiful,' she told him, worshipping his magnificent body with eyes and hands and mouth, 'so beautiful... You make me feel like Helen of Troy and Cleopatra and Barbara Castlemaine... How did I ever exist without this?'

And he laughed lazily, and called her a little sensual-ist, and made slow, ardent love to her until she thought she would drown in excitement, die of it, lose her mind to the skill and grace he brought to lovemaking, the fas-cination of his lean hard-muscled body as he showed her how responsive her own could be.

When, exhausted, they lay sprawled together on her bed, she said in a drained voice, 'Did I tell you that I've applied for a new job as regional co-ordinator?'

'Think you'll get it?'

She spread her fingers through the damp hair on his chest, pulling gently at the short, tangled strands. 'I don't know. I can certainly do it. At least my application shows that I'm willing.'

'When will you know?'

'Oh, not for weeks.' For a few seconds she gloomed about the rate of progress, then brightened up. 'But the trip with the Prime Minister to the Pacific Islands next month should be fun. I'm feeling rather elevated about that. When poor old Stan Forsythe had the bad luck to develop glandular fever I didn't think for a minute they'd send me.'

'Clever girl,' he yawned lazily.

She yanked on the hair. 'Chauvinist!' she jeered, then squeaked as he hauled her on top of him.

'That hurt. Are you sorry?'

'Not in the least.' She lowered her mouth and began to kiss his throat, nuzzling into it, tracing its length with the tip of her tongue. He tasted good, he smelt erotically of warm, aroused male.

'I think perhaps I should make you sorry,' he said ju-dicially as he pulled her hard down on to him.

She gasped, and moved, enfolding him, taking his male strength into her. 'You are insatiable.'

'You wouldn't want me nearly so much if I weren't.'

He had to be joking; unfortunately she didn't dare tell him that she would love him if he were in a wheelchair, and then his hands moved to settle her more firmly on him and in the daze of excitement that ensued she no longer remembered what he had said.

A long time later he asked, 'When is the PM going to the Islands?'

She told him and he frowned. 'I have to go to America around that time.'

As it turned out, he would be arriving back in New Zealand the day before Venetia would be leaving.

'Oh, damn,' she wailed when he told her.

He gave her one of his searching looks. 'What's the matter?'

The matter was that that very night was her cousin Elizabeth's twenty-first birthday. Perhaps because of his childhood Ryan had an almost romanticised view of the way families should behave towards each other; if he knew about Liz's birthday he might think Venetia should spend the evening with her, when all she would want to do was be with him. Still, Elizabeth would understand. Venetia and she had a pleasant, relaxed affection for each other.

'Nothing,' she said lightly. 'Just that it will be nearly a month without you.'

He said nothing, and she felt sudden fear claw at her with poisoned talons. She loved him so much, and knew so little about him except that he was necessary to her and she was not to him; she was a pleasant adjunct to his real life. But after a minute the odd tension in him dissipated and he gave her his lazy smile and her fears were dissipated in a wave of love.

After he left her Venetia wrote a long and very funny letter to her father's mother who lived in Sydney in Australia. Edith Gamble was a tough little woman who had passed her particular brand of blonde good looks to her sons and through them to her two granddaughters, and she and Venetia kept up a vigorous correspondence much enjoyed by both sides. Writing to her helped take Venetia's mind off her fears.

The night before Ryan left for America they stayed at home and had a sybaritic little feast in front of the fire, they spent long hours making love in the flickering firelight; when at last the exquisite release of tension came Venetia found tears on her face and tears in her heart.

'What is it?' Ryan asked gently, touching his tongue to a silvery trail.

'I don't know.' She stifled a sob and turned her face into the heated skin of his shoulder. 'I'm going to miss you.'

'I'll miss you, too.' He sounded almost tender, but when she opened her eyes there was a hint of wariness in his expression which ripped her euphoria into shreds.

But she smiled and enticed him into bed, and for a while it seemed that he might stay the night. When he left, about two o'clock in the morning, she turned her head into the pillow and wept again, shaken by secret fears.

The ten days passed, albeit slowly. She was disappointed to be refused the job she had applied for, but not surprised. She spent some time choosing her cousin's birthday present, finally settling on an exquisitely embroidered linen table-cloth; Elizabeth collected such things for her trousseau. On the night before the birthday she took the parcel to the neat, wooden house in the suburbs where her cousin still lived with her parents.

'I'm not opening it until tomorrow,' Elizabeth told her with an anticipatory squeeze of the parcel, shaking back the long hair which made her look like a fairytale princess.

'But I won't be here.'

Elizabeth looked disappointed but it was her mother who said, 'Oh, Venetia, why not? Surely for your cousin's twenty-first . . .? It's not as though we see much of you at any time . . .'

Venetia could have fabricated an assignment. The excuse would have been grudgingly accepted, but she did not lie. 'Sorry,' she said firmly, wishing that she had not been such a disappointment to her aunt. Janice had given her dead brother-in-law's child a home and had tried to be a mother to her, but she had never understood her.

'But what on earth is more important to you than Elizabeth's birthday?'

'Mum!' That was Elizabeth, sweet and kind as ever. Over the years she had become an expert mediator between her mother and Venetia. 'Honestly, it doesn't matter. We're not having a party, we're just going out to dinner, and if Venetia has another date, well, that's fine.' She bent and kissed Venetia's cheek. 'Thanks,' she said softly.

She made Venetia feel about two feet tall. In the chequered days of childhood Venetia had resented her because Elizabeth was calm and lovely and lovable, while she had been prickly and reckless and hot-tempered. Now she liked her immensely, although they had very little in common. Elizabeth was a teacher, a willowy thing four inches taller than her older cousin, and although they resembled each other her temperament was written in her serene face.

'Think nothing of it,' Venetia told her wryly, picking up her bag. 'I'd better go, it's getting late.'

Elizabeth came to the door with her. Outside, in the cool spring night, heavy with the scent of pink jasmine, Venetia said on a sigh, 'Sorry, Liz.'

'You're still the only person to call me that. Don't worry, it's all right. You've always been our maverick, that's the way we like you, bursting into our placid lives with all of the glitter and excitement of a comet. Have fun.'

'I intend to,' Venetia said, laughing, all of her anticipation suddenly blazing in her face, so that her cousin took a startled breath, a little envy spiking her voice as she replied, 'Well, if he's that special...!'

'He's—everything,' Venetia said starkly.

'Good luck, then. Dare I hint to Mum that there might be the prospect of wedding bells?'

'You may not! It's too early yet.'

And Ryan was not that sort of man, she thought as she drove away. Marriage might never be on his agenda. No, that was hardly positive thinking! One day he must learn to love her, but she certainly wasn't going to spoil what they had by hinting at marriage before he was ready.

She went to bed in a fever of anticipation which reminded her of her childhood, and her constant cry, 'I can't wait for it to happen!' Her aunt had always told her that time was something she couldn't hurry. You would think, she told her silent bedroom and empty bed, that I'd have learned that lesson by now.

Finally sleep claimed her, and the next day she went to work, and at lunch time there was a phone call.

'What are we doing tonight?' Ryan asked in that deep, half-mocking voice which sent shivers down her spine.

'I thought we might have dinner at my place,' she offered tentatively.

His amusement was patent. 'Have you got in caterers?'

'No, and my cooking's not that bad!'

'Darling, your cooking is about as basic as anything can be and still be called cooking. I'll reserve a table for us at Flamingo's. Be ready by seven. I promise we won't linger over the meal.'

She could almost see the sensual glint in his eye as he spoke. 'OK,' she said, her happiness lilting in her voice. 'I missed you.'

'Did you now?' He still sounded amused, as though the wasteland where his absence had marooned her was a pleasant, easily traversed place. She had to be careful not to tell him how wrong he was, because she was afraid that if she became at all possessive or dependent he would cut her out of his life as efficiently as a surgeon wielding a scalpel.

Her frown dissolved into a dreamy smile. Time, she thought, hugging herself, was on her side. Time, and the powerful physical magic which bound them together ever more tightly each day. And the communion of minds, the fact that they could talk for hours and never bore each other—oh, soon he would realise that he loved her!

She chose a dress in ivory silk, its sophisticated style lending her maturity and poise. The pastels which Elizabeth wore looked well on her too, but the soft, pretty colours made her resemble a little girl, and she wanted to be beautiful and worldly for Ryan.

Very carefully she made up, emphasising her eyes so that they gleamed gold fire between her lashes, sprayed her pulse spots with her favourite perfume, *First* de Van Cleef & Arpels, its warm blend of floral and spicy notes perfectly enhancing her heightened sense of expectation. The sandalwood and jasmine fragrance floated gently around her as she viewed herself with sudden anxiety in the mirror.

Her mouth was trembling and tender, like a young girl's in the throes of her first love affair; in spite of her attempt at sophisticated elegance she looked vulnerable and very, very young, almost virginal, she thought with an expression of faint disgust. Perhaps the ivory had not been the right choice, but it was too late. The doorbell was already sounding its imperative summons.

He was dressed in a dark lounge suit, the fit and colour highlighting his saturnine elegance; he looked at her for a long, silent moment, and she shivered suddenly at the wild blaze of emotion which kindled into life in the depths of his eyes. 'You are nice to come back to,' he said softly, and smiled. 'So nice that I don't think I'd better kiss you, or we'll never get out.'

'I had a large lunch.' Keep it light, she adjured herself as her hungry heart feasted on his presence.

'But I need more than you for dinner.'

She smiled at him with slow promise and said, 'Just so long as you don't sate yourself...'

'The last weeks have shown me that it's impossible for me to become sated,' he said a little sardonically. 'You are a woman of infinite variety. Now, let's get going.'

So, valued and happy as she had never been before, it seemed that the tangled threads of her life were at last braided together to form a pattern of beauty and worth.

And yet, in two short hours, she had to watch helplessly while the pattern unravelled into chaos and bitter desolation.

It happened so smoothly. As the waiter preceded them across the room Ryan bent to murmur in her ear, 'It looks as though someone is trying to catch your attention.'

Warned by no presentiment, she followed the direction of his dark gaze, ignoring the open appreciation in the gaze of a woman sitting close by. And there were her aunt and uncle and Elizabeth.

An odd little chill touched her heart. She hesitated, then altered direction, saying flatly over her shoulder, 'My family,' resenting the tentative smiles they were giving her.

'Your sister is very like you,' Ryan said softly. His eyes were absorbed, almost startled, as they rested on the pure, pretty contours of Elizabeth's face.

Incredulously Venetia realised that he was holding his elegant body tensely, as if under threat. She said crisply, 'Liz is my cousin. What you are seeing is the effect of good, strong Gamble genes.'

'Somehow,' he observed on an aloof note, 'I got the impression that they lived some distance away.'

Why, oh *why* hadn't she told him that her aunt and uncle lived in Auckland? Now she was condemning herself out of her own mouth as a woman who cared as little for her family as his mother had done. His face hardened and she thought she saw a flicker of contempt darken his already dark eyes.

While she made the introductions she reminded herself fiercely that he preferred experience and sophistication in his women. Men as worldly as Ryan were not attracted to sweet little virgins. He had said often enough that he admired her determination, the intensity with which she lived; she knew that he relished her wild abandon to passion, her inventive, intuitive knowledge of the ways he liked to be pleasured, as well as the sharp-edged intellect that met and matched his.

But deeper than logic were her women's instincts, and she reacted to a threat she still didn't accept with a woman's fierce possessiveness.

'Why don't you join us?' Elizabeth asked shyly. 'It's my twenty-first birthday today.'

Ryan smiled at her and Venetia stiffened. When he said yes without even consulting her, she had to try very hard to pretend that his acceptance was not both frightening and infuriating.

The last ten days had eaten into the fabric of her self-sufficiency; she had looked forward to this night with a passion which burned hungrily through her body and mind.

But she smiled, and sat down, and answered Elizabeth's thanks for the lovely table-cloth with a careless, 'I thought you'd like it. Liz,' she told Ryan, 'is into nest-building in a big way. Her Mr Right is going to be Mr Lucky too.'

Ryan slanted her a deliberate look, his impassive expression easing into a smile as he asked Elizabeth, 'And is this lucky man on the horizon?'

It was a perfectly innocent question, faintly indulgent, gently teasing. So why was Venetia assailed by a strong foreboding of disaster?

Elizabeth blushed and said quietly, 'No, I'm not as committed to my career as Venetia, but I'm not in a hurry to get married.'

Clearly it was the right thing to have said. Her parents beamed proudly, and Ryan smiled and Venetia felt a sick fear almost overwhelm her. Elizabeth was naturally reserved, but she could not hide her easy blushes or the way her hands trembled when Ryan spoke to her.

It was impossible to tell what Ryan was thinking. He charmed the older Gambles effortlessly, with almost insolent ease, his saturnine visage revealing only what he wanted. But Venetia's instincts were sharpened by love and desperation, and she sensed that the weight of his attention was directed at her lovely, serene cousin.

The realisation goaded her into stupid panic so that she found herself behaving like the sort of woman she had always derided, doing all the stupid little possessive things that tried to stake a claim.

She had been guilty of making plans—she, who had known from childhood that to plan for happiness was to kill it, sight unseen. Now, every sense preternaturally alert, she strove for balance in a world suddenly without foundation.

Fool, fool, to believe that time was on her side; she could see it running out, ebbing back over the desert that was her life, washing away all that was worthy, all the joy and love and ecstasy and the intensely satisfying friendship. She had been living in a fool's paradise. And tomorrow she was going away from him for two weeks.

It was this thought that towards the end of that dreadful evening impelled her to her feet, a smile pinned to her stiff lips as she said, 'Won't be a minute. Come with me, Liz.'

Although she kept her eyes firmly averted from Ryan she could feel his dark glance on her. Janice made to get up, only to subside with apprehension written large on her features as her husband made a quick little gesture of negation. Venetia wanted to rage and shout, she wanted to vent the words of despair and frustration forming on her tongue, but all she could do was precede her cousin towards the cloakroom.

Once safely behind the door, they had to wait before two women made their way out, shooting curious glances at them all the way, before Venetia said sharply, 'Don't look at me as though I'm going to tear your hair out!'

Elizabeth wouldn't meet her eyes. She turned to the mirror and began to pat her hair, saying in a half-hearted manner, 'As though you would!'

'Oh, I could, make no mistake about that.' Grimness made her voice stark. 'But you are family.'

'I don't know what you mean.'

Venetia took her lipstick from her bag and carefully applied it. Her gaze moved from her own reflection to that of her cousin. 'We're very alike, you and I,' she said reflectively. 'You are prettier, and taller, but we have almost identical features, thanks to Gran Gamble. Your eyes are pure green and mine are nearer yellow, but the shape is the same. So's our hair. It would probably be quite difficult to find another two cousins in the country as alike as we are. Ryan is important to me, Liz.'

'I don't know what——'

Venetia interrupted ruthlessly. 'Yes, you do.'

'Is he in love with you?'

'Yes,' she lied without hesitation, holding her cousin's eyes in the mirror with the hard insistence of hers. 'We share something very special.'

'Are you—well, are you living together?'

Venetia observed Elizabeth's heightened colour with concealed fear. 'No, we both need independence at this time, but we are lovers.' She allowed a hint of reminiscent passion to wind lazily through the words. 'Very ardent lovers.'

The colour in Elizabeth's cheeks deepened. She made a production of applying her own lipstick. 'In the best modern manner. You always were a rebel.'

Venetia's smile held more than a hint of cynicism. 'Nowadays,' she returned drily, 'determined virgins like you are the rebels. I don't want to have a fight, Liz, but if I must, I will, and I can fight very dirty. Don't look for special favours just because you happen to be my cousin. Ryan belongs to me.'

'I don't go round breaking up couples,' Elizabeth told her with the dignity which Venetia had always envied. 'Anyway, he's too sophisticated for me. That edge of danger might excite you, but it frightens me. Still, I'm rather flattered that you think I'm enough of a threat to give me the gypsy's warning!'

However, the rest of the evening proved that she had taken heed of Venetia's words. She didn't hang on to everything Ryan said with bated breath as she had before, and there was a definite reduction in the number of shy, appealing glances in his direction. Venetia was still tense, still plagued by uneasiness, but she was able to relax a little, striving to be her usual sparkling self.

She thought she had succeeded until at last she and Ryan were back inside her flat, and without preamble he asked, 'Don't you get on well with your family?'

She didn't want to talk. During the long, wearing evening the intolerable hunger he roused in her had been building until she was almost desperate with it. Now she slid her arms around him and pressed her face into his chest, inhaling his clean masculine scent with open and abandoned delight. Beneath her cheek she felt the pace of his heart begin to pick up.

'Venetia?'

She lifted her face to his determined, slightly impatient one. Angered though she was by her family's intrusion into her own personal idyll, she knew that look.

'They see me as a cuckoo in their conventional little nest,' she told him, searching his face with shadowed eyes. He was so beautiful, she thought achingly, so heart-stoppingly attractive, with the angular strength of his features an outward expression of the brilliant, powerful mind. Quickly, too brightly, she finished, 'I'm very fond of them, but we don't have much in common.'

He ignored the invitation in her voice, in her face, in the tentative movement of her slender body against his. With hands resting loosely on her shoulders he watched her from keen, narrowed eyes. 'It's a pity they don't mean much to you. I liked them.'

She knew little more of his life as a child than she had learned on the Sutherlands' yacht, but she read condemnation in his attitude and remembered the little boy who had been neglected in many subtle ways.

Quietly, almost sadly, she said, 'I like them too.'

'Yet you ignored your cousin's birthday.'

He seemed quite objective, the deep crisp voice coloured only by mild interest, but she was panicked into reacting sharply, pulling away with an angry, glittering smile. 'What is this, an inquisition?'

He looked down into her tense, vivid face, his own enigmatic. 'Perhaps I'm trying to find out what makes you tick.'

'Why? Is it so strange that I prefer you to my family?'

Damn, damn, damn, that was not what she wanted to say! More than anything else she wanted to recall her words, to start the whole wretched evening over. He had only just arrived home, tomorrow she was leaving him for a fortnight, and here they were almost quarrelling!

He smiled, with irony, and a gleam of desire fired the dark eyes. 'As always,' he said smoothly, 'you're right, my lovely little sensualist. Come to bed. Do you realise it's been ten long nights since I held my own personal houri in my arms?'

He made up for those lonely nights; like the houri he called her she gave him everything he asked for, flaming into vivid, uninhibited life under the primitive spell of his sexuality, giving until she was wrung dry and fell asleep in his arms, wondering how it was that a man so clever didn't know that she loved him.

When she woke she was alone. Just once, she thought wistfully, she would like to find him with her when she opened her eyes to a new day. The way he always left her seemed to typify their affair: passionate yet detached, as though the important part of his life was kept separate from her. Yet he could be tender, and was often kind; until last night she had hoped that he was coming to see her as more than a willing mistress. She rolled over and yawned, peering through half-opened eyes at the clock. She had time, plenty of time...

Now, running a hand down her body, she gloried in the tender skin, the slightly sore muscles, and memories of the violence of his passion. Last night he had imposed savage demands on her, using her body with a searing intensity which carried her to heights she had never before attained.

In return her love had propelled her response along inventive new channels until he had lost control completely, gasping her name in a paean of agonised ecstasy at the moment when she cried his, for a time banishing the fears which had torn so mercilessly at her.

Surely he could not, she thought a little desperately, have taken her with such obsessive desire if he had been attracted to Elizabeth. How stupid she had been last night, over-reacting like a desperately insecure woman to Elizabeth's interest in him.

To think that on the way home from the restaurant she had decided that she would pass up this trip to the Islands! It would have ruined her career to cry off, and for no more reason than the foolish fears of a woman in love. She had trusted him to be faithful to her while he was away, she would trust him to be faithful now.

Just before she left for the airport he rang and wished her a good trip, and she found her voice trembling as she made some mild joke. She cleared her throat and said urgently, 'I have to go. Miss me, won't you?'

'Of course I will,' he said.

Was he a little impatient? I hate this, she thought, blinking back sudden, stinging tears. 'Goodbye, darling.'

'Goodbye. Enjoy yourself.'

The tour was exhausting and exhilarating and exciting, something not to be missed, but on the last day she was contacted by her boss and sent on to one of the small democracies in the Western Pacific which had been devastated by an out-of-season hurricane. Ruthlessly calling in favours, she had managed to get there on an Air Force relief plane.

Once there she was so appalled by the devastation that she offered her services, and in between filing reports and cajoling her way on to relief expeditions worked long hours in the hospital until one of the endemic bacteria struck her down. She was lucky; it wasn't too fierce, but it delayed her departure for home so that she had been away three times as long as she had expected to be.

When at last she unlocked her front door she was so glad to be home that her small face seemed to glow with radiance. The long absence had clarified her emotions, helping her to admit that she was irrevocably bound to Ryan, her whole heart held in fee.

She rang his office, and was told by the bland voice of his secretary that he was in conference. Venetia pulled a face, but said, 'Can you tell him that I'm back, please,' smiling only when his secretary promised to do that.

He rang about ten minutes later, sounding preoccupied. 'I'll be around in about an hour,' he said after a swift exchange of greetings.

'Fine, that gives me time to have a shower.'

In fact she had just finished when the bell pealed urgently. Auckland was turning on a magnificent summer, and Venetia had pulled on a sundress she bought in Western Samoa. Straightening the fitted little bodice she flung open the door, excitement flaming her eyes to gold.

'Ryan! Oh, darling...'

She flung herself at him but although his arms caught her she detected the almost imperceptible stiffening of rejection. Immediately every repressed suspicion sprang free of its bonds. Only pride held her upright; she stepped back and looked up into his shuttered features.

'Hardly a rapturous reception,' she said, pain making her reckless. 'What's the matter?'

He said quietly, 'It's over, Venetia.'

She lifted a hand and touched the hollow in his throat where his pulse beat fast and heavy. In a still little voice she asked, 'Is it?'

He took a visible grip on himself, but he made no attempt to soften the blunt impact of his words. 'You'll probably always be able to make me want you, but that's all. You knew it was no great romance. We enjoyed each other, and now there's an end to it. Let's not part bad friends.'

'Why? Because it might make trouble in the family?' She read confirmation in the wary surprise in his eyes. 'I'm afraid Elizabeth can't have everything her own way,' she said tightly. 'Sweetness and light may be her style, but it's not mine.'

'Try for a little dignity,' he advised distastefully.

A chill crawled over her skin. Don't faint, she commanded through the distant drumming in her ears. Aloud she flung at him, 'She's going to want marriage, you know. She's the sort who has to have guarantees.'

His expression barely changed from the disciplined authority he used as a mask, but in the tense contraction of facial muscles too small to really see she read his in-

tention as if he had shouted it to the world. Not only
Elizabeth wanted marriage; Ryan was determined on it.

Deep inside Venetia something precious, something
fragile and infinitely beautiful shattered as though he had
robbed her of warmth and joy and self-respect.

She needed to hurt as she had been hurt to prevent
herself from shattering into as many pieces as her dreams.
Using all of her will-power to draw a deep sobbing
breath, she taunted bitterly, 'We'll see how ready she is
to marry you after I've told her what to expect. She's led
a very sheltered life, she has no more idea of how to cope
with appetites like yours than a kitten. My aunt has
brought her up to believe that sex is not quite nice——'

'If you do, or say, anything to hurt her,' he promised
with silky menace, 'I'll make you sorry that you were ever
born. I mean it, Venetia. I know you well enough to
understand where you'd hurt most.'

Idiot. Couldn't he see that he was killing her now?

'It would,' she hissed through her teeth, 'be worth it.
Whatever gave you the idea that I was a generous loser,
Ryan?'

She should have been terrified by the icy rigidity of his
features, but she was beyond control, goaded by anguish
into madness.

Ignoring the ominous way his hard mouth tightened,
the bitter fury that flared to life in his eyes, she went on
cruelly, 'Poor Liz, she'll be shocked out of her conventional little mind! Shall I tell her how you like——'

He made a snarling sound deep in his throat. Too late,
she tried to step back out of his reach, but he caught her
and crushed the words into oblivion on her lips.

The open, ruthless statement of her intention had
broken through his awesome self-control, pushing him
past the invisible limits he put on his temper. His hands
bruised her upper arms, clenching on to the soft flesh as
he imposed his strength on her in an embrace of raw,
unmatched power. At first Venetia resisted the savage

thrust of his tongue, but almost immediately the heightened tension of her emotions took over in a heated, silent sexuality which rendered what followed inevitable.

The little sunfrock was discarded and he followed her down on to the carpet, straddling her as he held her prisoner with his knees. She laughed, excitement sparking from every nerve-end at the surge of colour which flared across the bold sweep of his cheekbones. He tore his clothes off and she smiled as he removed the narrow bikini pants she wore with one swift fierce movement.

He used her roughly, careless of her pleasure, but she took fire and catapulted them both into an ecstasy like nothing either had ever experienced.

When it was over he collapsed, gasping, and she said in a drained voice which couldn't hide her triumph, 'Liz is not going to be able to give you that.'

He pulled himself free from her, and got into his clothes, looking down at her small sprawled figure with an icy, bitter contempt which froze through her body in a humiliation of despair.

'Accept it, it's over. And if you say anything to Elizabeth I'll break you.'

Then he was gone, and she lay like a broken puppet on the floor, beyond weeping, beyond emotion, held in a stasis of agony by the cold restrained menace of his words.

CHAPTER FOUR

THE bed was warm and comfortable, but Venetia woke from the nightmare with a rigid body and the faint memory of tears. After a long period, during which her heart calmed down as she realised that she was safe and that she had not spoken to Ryan since that evening almost six years ago, she leaned over and switched on the light. Three-fifteen in the morning.

The last time she had suffered through the dream had been two years ago; she had hoped her subconscious had relinquished it. She could never remember exactly what she dreamt, only that she roamed a wasteland of fear and bitter cold, but it always left her wrung out and shaky with no possibility of sleeping again that night, the unwilling victim of her brain's obsessive reluctance to let the past die. With determined cheerfulness she told herself that every two years was not so bad. When she had first come to share this house with her grandmother it had made her sleep hideous almost every night.

Wearily she climbed out of the high, old-fashioned cedar bed, listening with a part of her brain to the noises of an Australian night. It was over, six years over, and she was no longer in love with Ryan. Unfortunately, she had discovered during those six years, it was easier to learn not to love than to rid yourself of nightmares.

Downstairs she filled the kettle and plugged it in, and while she waited for it to boil she touched with the tip of her finger the unwitting cause of the dream's reappearance. Her aunt's writing was neat and easy to read. Even upside down the words were easily discernible.

Now that Gran Gamble is dead, there's no need for you to stay in Australia. I know you're working on your next novel, but you could do that just as well here, especially as you say it is set in New Zealand. We miss you very much.

A cynical little smile pulled in the corners of Venetia's mouth. It was Elizabeth her aunt missed, Elizabeth, who had died over a year ago of a swift and deadly leukaemia. Two days later Gran Gamble had at last given up her battle with old age. Venetia, who had been nursing her grandmother, had been unable to get over to see her cousin before she died.

The bubbling of the kettle put an end to her thoughts; she made the tea and poured it, and sat down at the kitchen table, eyeing her reflection in the uncurtained window opposite. She looked no older. Good genes, Gran Gamble used to say, and she was right. When the old lady had died she had looked two decades younger than her almost eighty years.

At least she had been of age to die, not like Elizabeth. Venetia sighed softly, recalling the last time she had seen her cousin, five months after Ryan's brutal rejection. Within a month she had fled across the Tasman Sea to seek refuge with her grandmother, and backed by that brisk, indomitable little woman she was trying to pick up the pieces of her life.

The sound of Elizabeth's laughing voice was the first either she or her grandmother had known of their approach; Venetia was trapped in the sitting-room as Elizabeth said at the front door, 'See, I told you, she never locks her doors in the daytime. Gran! May we come in?'

The breath exploded from Venetia's lungs. She clutched her grandmother's wrist, bruising the fragile flesh. Beneath her breath she begged, 'Don't tell them. *Please*!'

Edith Gamble sent her a sharp glance which softened immediately into compassion. 'Very well. Get into the sunroom. I'll make sure they don't go in there.'

She only just made it in time, hiding behind a screen in the furthest corner, her heart hammering so loud that she didn't hear the first part of the conversation.

It was Elizabeth's voice which penetrated her misery, smooth as cream, rich with fulfilment and satisfaction. 'Hawaii is *so* lovely,' she was saying. 'Ryan came up with the perfect honeymoon. We've had the most fabulous couple of weeks there, and I don't really want to go back home.'

The lazy, reminiscent words hurt Venetia more than whips on her skin. Wincing, she tried to cover her ears, but as though held by an evil enchantment she couldn't move, tortured by her inability to shut out the sound of her cousin's contentment.

'You both look well,' Gran observed.

'Oh, marvellous. We were so disappointed you didn't feel up to coming over for the wedding, so I thought I'd better bring Ryan in on our way back from our honeymoon to meet the matriarch of the family.' There was the tiniest pause before Elizabeth continued, 'Gran, is Venetia here?'

'She's staying with me, yes.'

'How is she?'

Edith paused, then said drily, 'She's well. She's helping me get my great-great-grandfather's diaries ready for publication, so she's kept quite busy. Why?'

'Is she—is she all right?'

'Why shouldn't she be? You know Venetia, she's not one who finds it easy to confide, but she seems well.'

Something in the autocratic old voice made Ryan say quickly and curtly, 'Elizabeth has a tender heart. She's been worrying.'

Venetia pressed her knuckles to her mouth. He sounded unbearably distant, as though he had not approved of Elizabeth's decision to come here. 'I hate him,' Venetia whispered fiercely, but she knew she lied. She had only to hear his voice...

Gran was not intimidated. Giving no quarter, she said with deadly blandness, 'I'm glad to hear that you have some small concern for her, Elizabeth. However, Venetia has courage, and enough character to cope with anything life throws at her.'

Venetia bit her lip in horror. But Ryan did not attack little old ladies, no matter how aggressive they were.

He said quietly, 'Perhaps you can convince Elizabeth of that.'

He had never been so protective of her, Venetia thought savagely. Oh, he had liked her, even felt some affection for her, but he had expected her to be able to look after herself. In that moment she was forced to accept that he really loved Elizabeth, and so took the first small step towards facing reality. Until then she had harboured secret, impossible dreams; now she knew that she had lied to herself, deluded, fooled herself. He loved Elizabeth.

Elizabeth was saying awkwardly, 'We parted bad friends. I feel—I hate that.'

Not giving an inch Edith retorted, 'I'm sorry about that, but we all have to face the consequences of our own actions sooner or later. If you haven't already learned that, Elizabeth, it's time you did. What happened between you and Venetia is a matter for your conscience, not mine. Now, tell me how your parents are.'

At last Venetia was able to drag her hands up to cover her ears so that the rest of the conversation was swamped by the dull roar of her own body echoes. She never knew how long they stayed, but when at last she heard the door close behind them she crawled over to the window and watched as they walked with her grandmother to the car.

They were an ideal couple, tall, elegant, her cousin's grace set off in contrast with Ryan's essentially male virility. They were holding hands; perhaps she could have read something into the fact that it was Liz who caught Ryan's hand in hers, but Venetia saw the smile he gave her, alight with a mocking tenderness, and she knew just how worthless all her dreams had been. Elizabeth was radiant, smiling into his face with such adoring wonder that Venetia turned away, unable to bear it.

She was sitting on the sofa when her grandmother came back. The older woman took one look at her pale face and made her a cup of tea; when she sat sipping it gratefully she said, 'So that's what happened,' adding crossly, 'Why didn't you fight for him, you silly girl? You've got a lot more to offer than your cousin, sweet though she is. He's too vital to stay content with her charming passivity for long.'

'He loves her,' Venetia said dully.

'Love? What's love? A mawkish sentiment without blood and backbone. He needs fire and passion and the excitement of the unexpected, and he's not going to find it in her. She'll stifle him. You've got guts, why didn't you go after him?'

Venetia's voice was heavy with resignation as she said, 'I did, but in all the wrong ways. You can't make a man love you, Gran. Ryan grew up in a house where both of his parents worked; his mother neglected him emotionally. I think he has this dream of a peaceful home with a wife whose sole aim is to keep it serene and loving, a dedicated mother and wife. You must admit Liz is ideal. She's sweet, and domesticated—and she was a virgin.'

'Oh, for heaven's sake!' Edith said robustly. 'Don't tell me he held that pathetic little marriage of yours against you!'

'No, oh no, but I suppose he assumed I'd had other affairs. He never asked, and I didn't tell him that before him there was only Sean.'

'It was no business of his. What man cares about virginity now? That sort of Victorian nonsense went out fifty years ago. Come to think of it, even the Victorians didn't bother about it! Plenty of widows remarried in Victoria's day.' She patted Venetia's hand. 'So, you were crossed in love. It's not the end of the world. He may be a very exciting man, but he's not the only one. You'll find yourself one you can trust, one who'll see behind that hard little mask to the tough but very worthwhile person behind it. And you'll discover that he'll love you without conditions.'

Venetia blew her nose and hugged her, comforted by her unsentimental outlook. Edith did not believe in self-pity; she was practical and positive and great fun. The ideal panacea for a broken heart.

Even now, after a year, Venetia missed her terribly.

As she drank her tea she frowned at the letter on the table. Janice said she had been ill, but she meant she was lonely. Janice was not the sort of person who made friends easily; for her, family took their place. She had often referred to Elizabeth as her best friend, and always told people that every woman needed a daughter. While Elizabeth was alive her mother had needed no one else.

The tea was suddenly bitter on Venetia's tongue. It was not Janice's fault that she could not accept how very little in common she had with her niece.

Venetia led a full, satisfying life in Australia; she had left New Zealand far behind. But even if she allowed herself to be persuaded back across the Tasman her aunt would be disappointed again. Janice liked to shop and lunch out, she enjoyed all of the feminine ways to fill in her time. Venetia was almost obsessive about keeping business hours and spent much of each day at her word processor.

She sat for a moment staring down at the dregs in her cup. Going back to New Zealand was impossible. Janice must know that. But knowing was one thing, accepting another. With a sigh Venetia took the cup and saucer across to the dishwasher and put them in it. Outside birds began to make the first soft morning calls; she listened for a few seconds before going back to her room to shower and dress.

When Edith Gamble had died she had left everything to Venetia, and that included as well as the house the ministrations of the daily, a dour, pleasant woman who worked silently and who had learned over the years that interruptions were most unwelcome, so that it was with considerable irritation that some hours later Venetia registered the fact that someone was knocking on the door of the study.

'Yes, what is it?' she called out a little impatiently, pushing a long tendril of blonde hair back from her face as she swivelled towards the door.

But it wasn't Mrs Edmonds who had knocked. It was Ryan Fraine who stood in the doorway, tall and dark and totally assured, hooded eyes enigmatic as they searched her face.

She sat very still for a moment. Then she said quietly, 'This is a surprise,' and got to her feet.

She was, she realised, dangerously close to fainting, but after she had supported herself for a moment on the edge of the desk the hideous whirling behind her eyes steadied then faded.

'Your aunt gave me your address,' he told her coolly.

Damn Janice with her manipulations and her selfishness! She knew, none better, why Venetia refused to come back. In fact, until Elizabeth died she had been most vigorous in her insistence that Venetia stay safely tucked away on the other side of the Tasman Sea.

Venetia tilted her face slightly away from that stabbing gaze, asking, 'Are you over here on business? Come into the sitting-room and we'll have coffee. What time is it?'

'Half past one.'

'Have you had lunch?'

'Thank you, yes.' Courteously he stood aside so that she could precede him through the door.

Stifled by his size and his nearness she led the way down the passage to the sitting-room. However, when he saw where she was planning to take him he said smoothly, 'I'll come with you and we can talk while you make the coffee.'

Clearly he was not going to give her a chance to recover herself. What did he think she would do, run away? Only once had she done that, and then only because she had others beside herself to consider; it was not going to happen again.

She should have felt a mild triumph at her appearance of calmness, but she was too strung-up; she wanted him out of the house as soon as possible, and she didn't care how she managed it.

'How long are you here for?' Yes, the water running into the kettle hid any unevenness in the tone of the words; her voice sounded just right, barely interested, cool. Above all, confident.

'That depends. I'm organising a film.'

'Ah, yes. Aunt Janice wrote that you had a new one under consideration. I must congratulate you on your skill as a producer and director. Three hits on your hands in the last three years, and all three praised by the critics! I believe the last one is doing exceptionally well in America.' She put the lid on the kettle and switched it on at the wall, then began to set out the tray. 'Still take your coffee black and sweet?'

'No sugar. Did you see *Fortitude*?'

'Like the rest of the world I thought it was wonderful.' She reached for cups and saucers, put them on the tray and took the milk from the refrigerator.

'You must know the feeling. Like the rest of the world I enjoy your books.'

She shrugged. 'Given the material I had to work with I could hardly fail. My great-great-grandfather had an exceptionally exciting life and a real talent for writing. The publication of his diary cashed in nicely on this modern fascination for our heritage and our past. And when I finished it I used the surplus material I'd gathered as background for the historical novels. It was exciting that they sold so well.'

'Profitable, too,' he said smoothly, and without pausing asked her how her latest one was coming on.

'It's finished bar the shouting. I'm still polishing, but it will be on its way in a few days' time.'

She made a little producton of pouring the boiling water over the grounds. The smell of coffee was fragrant in the quiet room. When that was done she turned away from his observant, inimical gaze towards the housekeeper, who had just appeared in the doorway, widening her eyes to convey what she hoped was a warning. Mrs Edmonds came further into the room; as she introduced them Venetia blessed the housekeeper's poker face, not for the first time.

Ryan smiled, all leashed, dangerous charm, shook hands, and made a comment which set Mrs Edmonds to the nearest thing to laughter which Venetia had ever seen. She waited her moment to ask, without any inflection other than the most casual, 'Would you mind ringing Mrs Dodwell and telling her that as I'm a little hung up this afternoon, I'll collect my parcel about five o'clock if that's all right with her.'

The smile fading into her normal severity, Mrs Edmonds said, 'I'll do that. Will you want me tomorrow?'

Venetia grinned. 'No, you can't get out of going to the dentist's like that. They don't hurt nowadays, you know.'

'Try telling my subconscious that.' Dour as ever, the older woman left them.

'She's terrified of the dentist,' Venetia explained chattily as she led the way into the sitting-room. She gestured towards a wide wing-chair which had been her grandfather's favourite and when Ryan was sitting down she said brightly, 'Now, tell me why you came to see me, Ryan. But before you do, tell me how Janice is. In her last letter she hinted at being unwell.'

Her hands were very steady as she poured the coffee and handed it to him, still very steady as she picked up her own cup and sat back in her chair. She looked enquiringly at him as though he was an old friend, with nothing stronger or more dangerous than liking between them.

The broad shoulders lifted in a shrug. He had been looking around her grandmother's pretty, old-fashioned room with its family photographs on the piano, but now his eyes came to rest on her face and she was impaled by his keen gaze, sharp and hard as a lance of obsidian. 'She misses Elizabeth,' he said bluntly.

Venetia nodded, despising herself for listening so hard to that deep voice, straining to discern any emotion when he said his dead wife's name. 'Yes, I know. I had a letter from her yesterday. She seems to have some strange idea that I might take Liz's place.'

'I'm sure she realises that that is impossible.' The hurtful words were delivered without any noticeable intonation. 'But would it be so difficult to go home?'

Impossible, as her aunt well knew. Aloud she said carefully, 'I've made a new life here, Ryan, one that I enjoy. I don't want to go back.'

'A man?' Her hesitation made him smile ironically as he answered his own question. 'Well, of course. When has there not been a man in your life? I see no signs of him around.'

Thank God for that.

'My private life is no concern of yours.' She hid her anger and a flash of fear by smiling politely, but all of the hazel had faded from her eyes, leaving them yellow as a cat's behind the thick fringe of her lashes.

'He's more important to you than your aunt? The woman who brought you up, who has always considered herself to be your mother?'

She sighed. 'Look, I realise that you must be concerned about Aunt Janice, otherwise you wouldn't stoop to moral blackmail, but if your mother asked you to go back to England, would you go?'

'No, but there is a slight difference. My mother has never needed me, and I was married. You are not.' His eyes, hard as quartz, held her reluctant ones in a glance from which there was no escape. 'Or is there a possibility of marriage? Are you engaged to this lover?'

Venetia couldn't hide the sarcasm which sharpened her voice. 'No.'

'I thought not,' he said with silky derision.

Venetia shrugged. There was a silence, taut with unspoken thoughts and the memories of old emotions, and then he said flatly, 'Had I realised that you would exile yourself like this I'd have been a little less cruel to you when we parted. I had no idea that your pride would demand such measures.'

She gave a twisted, ironic smile. 'I'm surprised that you allow me any pride. I thought you considered me the lowest of the low.'

'Don't be a fool. One thing I admired about you was your refusal to hide behind the hypocrisy that most people use to cloak their emotions and actions. You were sharp-edged and abrasive, but you were honest.'

'You understood very little about me,' she returned calmly. 'Actually, I left for several reasons, one of which was that Janice made it more than obvious that you would all be greatly relieved if I did so. Entirely understandable. Even your massive self-possession might have wilted a little if you were for ever falling over a discarded mistress. However, that's all past and has nothing to do with the fact that I'm not prepared to give up everything I have here on a whim of my aunt's. I notice that you have carefully avoided saying that she is really ill.'

He drained the coffee, his features chiselled sharp with exasperation and impatience. Venetia watched warily; she knew that look.

'So your answer is no,' he said after he had set the cup down.

She nodded, small but indomitable. 'I'm sorry.' And was racked with fresh anger at her aunt's manoeuvrings.

'You won't need to see much of me, if that's what's worrying you.'

'Six years is a long time,' she said, smiling wryly. She didn't even realise that she was evading the issue until his taunting smile made her flush. Then, goaded, she lied, 'Your presence in New Zealand has nothing to do with my refusal to go back. You no longer affect me in any way.'

And that, she thought with bitter satisfaction, should hammer it home.

He smiled in turn, but his was the reaction of a reckless man to a challenge, and he came out of the chair with the dangerous smoothness of a predator's rush to the kill. Venetia flinched back into her chair, her eyes wide with dismay and astonishment as he took her cup and saucer and set them down on the table. Then his hands fastened just above her elbows and she was pulled to her feet with insulting, implacable insistence.

'Now just a——'

The words were smothered by the pressure of his mouth—predatory, determined to make a point. She refused to surrender, clamping her lips together to deny him access, so his hand slid beneath her arm and closed cruelly around the soft curves of her breast.

To her horror Venetia felt an uprushing of the incandescent desire which she thought had died long ago. Rigid, furious though she was with him, her mouth softened beneath his. He lifted his head and watched her, his smile twisted and mocking;.

'Damn you,' she muttered through clenched teeth.

Ryan laughed deep in his throat.

Revulsion warred with the heated, desperate sensuality she had tried so hard to forget. At least she was the one to pull away. It hurt, but she could feel the unmistakable signs of his arousal and suddenly the forbidden pleasure was gone, replaced by shame and anger and fear. She clamped down on all three, aware that if she gave in to any of them she was going to be easy prey for him.

He let her go and stood watching her with narrowed eyes, the dark flush of desire licking along his strong cheekbones, his mouth a hard line. But it was a weary triumph which flamed behind his lashes.

Venetia touched her finger to her sore top lip. It took extreme will-power before she could say steadily, refusing to grant him more than that minor triumph, 'It seems I was wrong, at least in one respect.'

'What other respect was there ever between us?' He spoke with contempt, but he couldn't hide the tell-tale unevenness in his tones, and for a wild moment her heart rejoiced. Until every instinct gained by feminine forebears during aeons of being the weaker sex screamed a warning, and she stepped away from him, automatically smoothing hair which had somehow become tangled across her forehead. 'You've just given me another reason for not going back,' she said steadily. 'I'm not terribly well equipped to handle rejection.'

'There need not be any rejection.'

She stared at him, her face slowly paling as her brain took in the implications. 'That's sick,' she whispered after long, tense moments. 'I'm not going to take my cousin's place in your bed. Or your life.'

He laughed without humour, suddenly blazing with danger, his dark eyes sardonically appraising the taut antagonism she was projecting. 'Why not? She had no such inhibitions.'

Astonished more by the ragged note in his voice than his words she could only stare at him. He met her gaze with sardonic challenge as he went on, 'Don't worry, I've accepted her death and mourned her and got over it. And you're right, that was a mistake, I have no desire to go back six years, but you shouldn't go round throwing out challenges. I find it hard to resist them.'

She eyed him uncertainly, aware that he had exerted his formidable self-control to rein in an impulse which he was angry at having loosed.

'Oh, sit down,' he said tiredly, 'I'm not going to leap on you. Do you want to know why I got your address from your aunt and came to see you?'

She said slowly as she sank back into the chair, 'No. I have a feeling I'm not going to like it.'

He lifted his brows. 'One thing I would never have accused you of is cowardice.' But he paused as if to collect his thoughts before he began, 'Do you remember selling the film rights of your book? The first one, your grandfather's diary?'

'Yes. But it wasn't to you. It was to a company.'

'Quick as ever,' he taunted. 'The company is my holding company. And that is the film I'm setting up.'

She sat stunned, unconsciously chewing on her bottom lip while she took it in. Vividly she remembered her exasperated agent's advice that she was being paid more than enough for the rights, that she was crazy to hold out for editorial supervision of the script. The spokesman for the company had been a little testy, but when she had made it quite clear that she was not going to relent he had given in. If he was Ryan's front man it was no wonder he had been reluctant!

'Then why are you over here?' she asked carefully.

'For obvious reasons. You demanded editorial supervision of the script. I've come to work on it with you.'

He was laughing at her, she realised, mocking the dismay he saw in her expression with a savage amusement. Abruptly she got to her feet and paced across to the window, her slender body stiff with anger and defiance. After a moment's concentrated thought she swung around and said crisply, 'All I want is supervision. I'm damned if I'll write the thing for you. When I made that stipulation it was because I didn't want some idiot director to turn Albert Gamble into another cardboard swashbuckler. He certainly lived like an adventurer, but he was much more than a nineteenth-century Errol Flynn. If you're directing it I'll waive my rights.'

His brows drew together in a quick frown. She had, she realised with stark satisfaction, surprised him. But when he spoke it was with that mocking note in his words. 'Do you trust me that much, Venetia?'

'I've never questioned your professional integrity.'

He smiled cynically. 'That sounds more like you. However, I'm not prepared to run the risk that you might wait until the film is done and then insist on changes. Or sue. So I'll want your supervision.'

His refusal to trust in turn hurt, but she subdued it. She knew little about film-making, but she was aware that budgeting could be a nightmare. So she said stiffly, 'Very well then, I'll accept that. You get the script done and I'll check it——'

'No, that will waste too much time. I want you available for consultaton, and to check on the accuracy as we go along.'

She gave him a long, hard look, a look which he met with a bland comprehension she didn't trust one bit. For some reason he had organised this; he wanted her to work closely with him for the weeks it would take to produce a script, and she was afraid. Surely, unlike her aunt, he was too well balanced to think that she might take Elizabeth's place in his life?

No, she was being stupid. He knew the difference between them, none better. Her cousin he had loved, while that kiss of a few minutes ago had proved that he lacked any respect for her. It had been a suffocating, demanding expression of mastery and lust, and it was to her eternal shame that she had gone up like wildfire.

Aloud she objected, 'I don't believe that you need my constant supervision at all. In fact, I think you're being bloody-minded about it. And I'm not going to give you an answer now——'

'You can have another look at that contract if you wish,' he interrupted indifferently, his eyes watchful, 'but it's watertight. You made sure of that.'

Impatiently she pushed her fingers through her hair. 'You can't want to stay here for the time it takes you to get the script right. Do you normally write the scripts for your films?'

'If I have to,' he said indifferently.

'Which ones have you done?'

She was trying to avoid making a decision, and he knew it, but he told her, mockery gleaming in his smile. '*Fortitude* and *A Severe Compulsion*.'

The scripts of both had been brilliant, taut and spare and subtle. She said woodenly, 'Oh,' and flushed at the unkind laughter in his expression. It incited her into saying angrily, 'Well, I'm not prepared to have you hanging around here. Go back and do the wretched script and send it over. Damn it, Ryan, I trust you to do it properly!'

His brow lifted at that. 'Do you? I'm rather touched—and very surprised.'

She stared at him, willing herself to say nothing.

Into the heavy silence the shrill summons of the telephone jerked her out of something perilously like panic. 'Excuse me,' she muttered as she went out into the hall to answer it.

It was Kay Dodwell. Without preamble she said, 'Venetia, I think you'd better come around straight away. That parcel of yours has developed spots!'

CHAPTER FIVE

VENETIA got rid of him immediately and without ceremony, simply stating that an emergency had come up. As soon as his hired car had turned the corner she drove the half-mile or so to Kay's house where she was met by two beaming, small boys, one of whom greeted her by lifting his T-shirt to display proudly a collection of spots on his chest.

'Chicken-pox,' Kay said succinctly. 'I've made an appointment for you at the doctor. She'll be able to give you something to stop the spots from itching so much. You're lucky, it's a mild case.'

'Oh, John,' Venetia said helplessly, ruffling the dark hair so like his father's. 'Of all the times to get a bug!'

The doctor prescribed a lotion for the itch and said in the matter-of-fact manner of a mother who is a realist above all, 'See if you can keep him in bed for a couple of days. You won't, of course, so make sure he's warm but not too hot, otherwise the blisters will drive him crazy. He's not going to get any sicker than he is now. Good luck.'

Venetia laughed and gave her son a wry, loving look. He grinned, enjoying the fuss, and took advantage of it to beg an ice-cream when Venetia picked up the prescription from the chemist.

'When Jamie is sick,' he said cunningly, 'Auntie Kay gives him ice-cream all the time.'

'Oh yes? I don't believe you, but as we're having ice-cream for pudding tonight we'll give it a miss now.'

He shot her a swift look. Although he still hated being crossed, he had almost overcome his tendency to the truly

fiercesome tantrums which had bedevilled him a year or
so ago; he contented himself now with a spirited plea for
grapes. Laughing, Venetia assented and watched with
doting eyes as he chose the exact bunch he wanted.

When he had completed the purchase he carried them
triumphantly off and in the car picked one of the berries
and offered it to her, chuckling as she made rude smacking noises to express her appreciation of the treat. At that
moment her heart overflowed; she looked at him and he
said uncertainly, 'You look mad, Mummy.'

'No, I'm just thinking.'

'Oh, about the book.' He was used to her habit of
daydreaming, accepting it as just another of her vagaries,
like her insistence on spotless hands.

Jolted, because she had been imprinting the strong arrogance of his father's features over his, and recognising
anew just how alike they were, she smiled tenderly at him.
John, too, had high, proud cheekbones and a chin which
expressed determination bordering on stubbornness.

She had no idea how Ryan would greet the news that
he was a father, but she was almost certain that if he
knew of his existence he would not turn his back on the
child. Which meant he would insist on visiting rights, and
that little episode in his arms had shown her just how
hazardous any contact with him could be. As soon as she
got home she was going to get that contract out of her
files and go over it with a fine-tooth comb.

Away from his dominating presence she had recovered much of her normal resolution, and she was determined not to be forced into writing the wretched script
with him. At any other time she would have been thrilled
at the knowledge that her book was to become a film, but
the fact that it was Ryan who owned the rights spoiled her
pleasure in her own achievement.

Back at home John climbed out of the car, clutching
his precious grapes and a large, highly coloured picture
of a striped cat which he had painted.

'I made the stripes red,' he told her, 'but Jenny Sanders said that I shouldn't've, 'cause it was a grey cat.'

He spoke with all the scorn of the avant-garde artist for the conventional, and Venetia hid a smile, saying soothingly, 'I think you were quite right.'

'Well, I know *that*.'

The key scraped in the lock at the exact same time that the hinges on the gate squeaked. She turned, and there was Ryan, his eyes on the child beside her, his facial muscles clenched so tightly that he seemed to be wearing a mask.

Venetia felt that all her worst nightmares had come true. She froze, watching with dilated eyes as child and man looked each other over with identical stares, the same straight brows drawn together in the same frown above two sets of eyes as dark as midnight, the boy already giving promise of attaining his father's lean height and grace of movement, both faces stamped with clearly defined features which had been formed from the same mould.

Venetia drew a painful breath before asking sharply, 'Have you had chicken-pox?'

Surprise flickered in Ryan's eyes. He lifted his brows but replied calmly, 'Yes, when I wasn't much older than——'

'John,' his son supplied, when he realised his mother wasn't going to give his name. 'John Ryan Gamble. I'm five years old.' He looked at his laden hands, set down the grapes with great care on the step and held out a grubby little paw.

Ryan shook it, saying with all of the formidable charm he could muster, 'How do you do? I'm Ryan Fraine.'

His son smiled with an equal amount of charm. 'Are you? Mummy, this man has the same name as me.'

'That's nice,' Venetia managed inadequately, aware that she had gone as pale as a wraith.

'Do you want a cup of tea?' John enquired politely. 'Mummy always has a cup of tea now. It's her life-saver.'

'Thank you,' Ryan said with rigidly controlled formality, still watching his son.

Venetia led the way into the kitchen, listening numbly to John's voice as he chattered away. She put on the kettle and with a muttered excuse whisked him away upstairs, grateful because Kay had bathed him. When he was tucked into bed with a small cluster of grapes and his adored panda bear he smiled sleepily at her, yawned, and asked blurrily, 'Why's that Mr Ryan here, Mummy?'

'Just business.' The words sounded as though they might splinter in her mouth, but he accepted them without question.

Lucky John, she thought grimly as she came down the stairs. It must be marvellous to have the unquestioning trust of a happy child that each new day was going to be better than the one before. Growing up shattered that faith as maturity brought with it the painful realisation that the opposite was just as likely to be true.

Ryan was waiting for her in the kitchen. He had made the tea and was leaning against the bench, his big body oddly relaxed for a man who must have suffered quite a shock. Venetia was surprised at the lack of fury in his expression; it sat oddly with her memories of the man. The Ryan she remembered would have gone for the jugular as soon as he realised what she had done.

His stillness made her very wary. Without saying a word he waited while she put cups and the necessary equipment on to a tray, and carried it into the sitting-room. Perhaps, she thought, he didn't care. Plenty of men adopted an insultingly casual attitude to any children from liaisons, managing to dismiss them as nothing more than nuisances, easily disregarded mistakes.

She might even have believed that, except that she could have sworn that Ryan was not one of them. Even if the unhappy circumstances of his childhood hadn't made him sensitive to children's needs, he possessed a rare empathy. What had made him an outstanding reporter, what gave his films their appeal, was the passionate concern which came across so strongly.

And there was a threatening quality to his silence which kept her tense while she poured the tea and handed him a cup.

He drank half of it, using her uneasiness to keep her off balance before asking softly, 'Why didn't you tell me?'

She shook her head. 'What use would it have been? You were married by the time I knew definitely.'

It was not exactly the truth, but she made it sound convincing. Not convincing enough, for he immediately said, 'I don't believe that. I—we were married five months after you left.' The pause was quite deliberate. 'You could have prevented that marriage by telling me.'

Sparks flashed in her eyes. 'Do you think I wanted you by then?' she demanded fiercely. 'You're not so irresistible. You had made it quite obvious what you thought of me, and you belonged to Elizabeth.'

He leaned back into the chair, fitting his broad shoulders into the wide wings. When he spoke his voice was judicial, completely lacking in emotion. 'You gave me no indication that you were anything but a sharp, clever woman, ambitious enough to think little about using your body to advance you in your job, with a modern attitude towards sex and morality. I enjoyed your company and your body and that was all you wanted from me in return. You never mentioned marriage. I thought that your unfortunate experience with the institution had put you off it.'

'It's not much use hankering after something you can't have,' she retorted sweetly. 'But I didn't tell you about John because I could see that you were in love with Elizabeth. I didn't need you. My grandmother was willing to provide a home for us. If I have to accept charity I'd rather it was from a member of the family.'

He nodded, surprising her. 'Yes, I understand that sort of pride. I also understand that it probably fed your ego to know that you had my son when Elizabeth was unable to conceive.'

The sneer made her feel ill. She drank some tea to ease the raw ache in her throat and said quietly, 'If that's what you think then I'm not going to attempt to defend myself. But just for your information, I was very fond of Liz. I'd like you to go, please.'

He sighed and said unexpectedly, 'I'm sorry, that was a lousy thing to say. Put it down to shock. But I have no intention of going, Venetia. I'm staying with you here while we work on this script together and then you and my son are coming back to New Zealand with me.'

She exploded into anger, jumping to her feet and advancing on him as if she would throw him out personally. 'I'll see you in hell first!' she swore, small hands clenched tightly at her side, antagonism bristling in her stance and her expression. 'Get out of here!'

'No.'

He spoke with a kind of bored determination, and when she stamped her foot in impotent fury he reached out a hand and hauled her into his lap, coolly subduing her writhing, twisting body until she was forced into stillness.

'Now listen to me,' he said in the silky tones she had heard in her nightmares. 'If you force me to take you to court I'll take everything you value from you in payment. Everything. Your son, your peace of mind, this life you've built for yourself...'

She said in a low voice, hating herself because it was surrender of a sort, 'No court would give you custody of John, and I wouldn't deny you access.'

He laughed and bent his head so that his breath played across the sensitive skin of her neck. 'Little mother, you don't know what a court would do. But I can assure you that I am not bluffing. And a court case like that would bring us all, but especially John, a most unwelcome amount of publicity.'

She winced and he said with easy irony, 'All you have to do is work on this script with me, and then come and live in New Zealand.'

He had to be bluffing. He *had* to be! But he never made empty threats. For a moment she toyed with the idea of daring him to do his worst, but he had too much on his side. He knew her too well. She could not let John become the centre of a custody battle. Although he was too young to understand, the experience would mark him for life. In her years as a reporter she had seen enough frightened, bewildered children torn between bitter parents to know that she would do anything to prevent her son from enduring such a trauma.

Suddenly she struggled, desperate to get away from him. When he let her go she could not look at him, but she felt the impact of his regard right across the room as she walked over to the sideboard. To her the old-fashioned room had always represented security, so she had made few alterations; it was almost exactly as it had been in her grandmother's time. Now she picked up a photograph in a silver frame and stared down at it. It was twenty or so years old, a studio portrait of her aunt and uncle with their family, sweetly smiling Elizabeth beside a reluctant Venetia, her eyes focused on something out-side the picture, wary as a caged eagle. They were alike enough to be taken for sisters. Even then Elizabeth had been tall for her age, matching her elder cousin inch for inch as they grew.

Frozen tears ached behind Venetia's eyes. She put the frame down and said tonelessly, 'You leave me little op-tion.'

'I've done you a favour,' he said with careless disdain. 'You can come home with all flags flying. You won't have surrendered.'

'No? You degrade me.' The words came out grittily, clipped with emotion.

Sparked by the intensity of her anger his reply came roughly. 'It's just as degrading for me to want a woman who'll sleep with any man who attracts her, but it's there, wishing won't make it go away.'

The deliberate, cold crudity of his words brought colour to her cheeks. She said raggedly, 'If you—if I let you stay, I don't want you to touch me.'

'Oh, I think that can be arranged. What I can get from you is fairly common currency, darling.' He stepped back and she turned to see an icy male satisfaction in his eyes.

She was beaten, she knew it, yet she had to go ahead with it. 'Very well,' she snapped. 'I'll see you in a week's time.'

'You'll see me tonight,' he told her calmly. 'In fact, this is it. My bag is out in my car.'

'But I have work to do on my book!'

'That's all right. You have a sick son, too.'

Some note in his voice made her stiffen. 'And what do you mean by that?'

'Why, nothing, except that it will be a perfect opportunity for John to get to know me. I can keep him out of your hair while you finish your all-important book!'

Anger tightened her mouth, flew banners of colour beneath her clear skin. She looked at him with a level, hard stare and said sharply, 'I love John very much. I do not neglect him in any way and I will not have you insinuating that I do.'

He said cynically, 'But your book comes first.'

'If there was any necessity for it I'd stop work on it to care for John. However, the doctor assured me that he won't get any sicker than he is now, and as you must have seen, that isn't very bad.'

'I'm sure you're right,' he said with poisonous smoothness.

He was not convinced. No doubt he would never believe that John was a normal, happy child, in no way scarred by the fact that she worked for a living. The discipline that her work imposed on him was not resented, was no threat to the security and love he took for granted, because her son knew that he was the most important person in his mother's life.

Ignoring his humourless smile she said maliciously, 'John doesn't need you to fill the empty spaces in his life, because there are none.'

'You still haven't learned to watch that tongue of yours,' he said, sounding bored. 'I think I could get heartily sick of it.'

'You know what to do about it.'

Ryan shook his head with deceptive amusement. 'My dear, you are the one who is going to suffer if we keep up a state of warfare. I don't give a damn, but I hope you're too good a mother to want our son to know how things are between us.'

She bit her lip, well aware of the threat behind the bland words.

'So be sensible,' he finished smoothly, his dark eyes glittering with cold mockery as they surveyed her flushed face and tense stance. 'As for the empty spaces in his life, you may not want to admit it, but there's one labelled "Father". I intend to fill it.'

Venetia gave him no reply, her mind swirling with inchoate, threatening suspicions. After a few moments she sat down and finished drinking her tea, her face revealing nothing of the thoughts which worried at her self-control. She no longer loved Ryan; how could she? His cruelty all those years ago had killed the love she had thought so eternal, but the physical attraction was as strong as it had ever been. Strong, and dangerous, because he felt it too; he was no more immune to it than she was.

Through screening lashes she looked at him, trying to find signs in the strong features of the years which had passed. There were a few more lines at the corners of the dark eyes, a tighter line to a mouth which had always been ruthlessly self-controlled, but apart from that time had left him curiously unscathed. He would wear well, of course. The magnificent bone structure he had bestowed on his son would make him eye-catching when he was eighty. Yet it was not his physical attributes, stunning though they were, not the lean, balanced body or the stretch of tanned skin over sculpted features which made women look at him. He possessed an effortless authority, a blazing vitality which drew all eyes. He stamped his own impress on the world about him. He was not a man to be liked, that was too anaemic a word. Certainly he could never be overlooked. One loved him, respected him, admired him. Once Venetia had loved him. Then she had hated him. Now, for her own survival she had to learn to be indifferent to him.

It was not going to be easy.

She asked suddenly, 'What did you mean when you said that I was prepared to use my body to advance my job?'

'Weren't you?'

She shook her head. 'There's nothing professional about that sort of behaviour. And even you admit that when it came to my job I was thoroughly professional.'

'What about Jeff Caldwell?'

She frowned. 'What about him?' she asked slowly.

He shrugged, his expression sardonic, almost weary. 'My dear, he made no attempt to hide the fact that you got your chance on television because you slept with him. Then there was Brett March. You gave me a rather touching tale about your marriage, but he told me that he'd had to pay you before you agreed to leave his cousin.

Presumably you were prepared to use the marriage to get away from smalltown life. And you certainly weren't slow about hopping into bed with me. I always presumed it was because you wanted a job on the news team of the station I was setting up. You probably would have been offered one if you'd stayed.'

Her lips felt swollen and stiff, but she managed a light, almost amused tone. 'You are too flattering.'

Incredibly his voice softened. 'I suppose it was because you had a hell of a lot of problems getting people to take you seriously. Once you got your chance no one could fault your work. You were totally professional.'

She said indistinctly, 'Thank you,' and wondered hysterically why she wasn't tearing his eyes out. How dared he think that she had slept her way up the ladder! How dared he accept vile innuendoes as truth! At that moment she knew what it must be like to murder in a red flare of rage, counting no cost. And then the fury ebbed away and she was left with the bitter taste of defeat in her mouth.

His assumptions explained a lot. No wonder he hadn't cared about her feelings. And her behaviour must have unwittingly reinforced his cynical assessment of her character.

She had behaved stupidly because she had loved him. But even if she had been the brittle, amoral woman he considered her she would have been wounded by his abrupt dismissal of her in favour of her cousin; strangely, it helped soothe her pride to understand at last why he had made no attempt to soften the blow.

He had been watching the subtle shift of expressions across her small face, his brows drawn together as though he did not understand her reactions. After a moment he said calmly, 'I wonder if we could declare a truce. We're going to be seeing a lot of each other, and it will be easier for John. After all, we shared some pleasant times, we enjoyed each other's company. There's no reason why what happened almost six years ago should be allowed to shadow any relationship we might form now.'

All very civilised, when she was feeling drained in the aftermath of a surge of completely primitive savagery. She could give him no reply and after a moment the cool, dispassionate voice continued, 'You know now that you won't win concessions from me by using your rather too desirable body. We understand each other. That could form quite a good basis for the future.'

He paused, obviously waiting for an answer and, when she gave none, continued in a harder tone, 'Give up any idea of running away again. I've missed out on enough of John's childhood. I don't intend to lose touch with him now.'

'I was going to contact you eventually,' she said without emotion. 'I just didn't know how to tell you.'

'So I saved you from thinking up a way.' It was quite clear that he didn't believe a word of it.

She had not been lying. John had the right to know his father, but she had been a coward and the longer she left it the harder it would have been for all of them. However, she had always intended that some day Ryan should know of his son.

Shrugging, she said in a toneless little voice, 'If you get your things from the car I'll show you your room.'

It was strange to make up the bed in the spare room knowing that Ryan would be stretching his lean length on it. She had never dreamed that he would find his way here; it had been a haven, a shelter when she had so desperately needed one. And now she was putting percale sheets on the bed and showing him where the bathroom was, even picking flowers from the garden to take away the formal, slightly stuffy atmosphere of all spare rooms.

'Where does John sleep?'

'Just along the passage.'

John had kicked the bedcovers off and was sprawled in his usual splendid abandon across the sheets, his face flushed with sleep and a slight temperature. Pandy was at his usual post, on the floor half way across the room. John muttered something as they came in and opened his eyes, then turned over and pushed his face into the pillow.

Venetia smiled and picked up the panda, tucking it beside her son. He said, 'Yes!' explosively without stirring and she looked up to see Ryan looking at her with a strange light in the black depths of his eyes.

Once outside he said, 'I never thought of you as being at all maternal.'

'Even the crocodile is credited with parental instincts,' she said acidly. 'If you'll excuse me, I'll see about dinner.'

He lifted his brows at that. 'Cooking, Venetia?'

'It's that or starve. The housekeeper leaves a meal so all I have to do is prepare the vegetables, and thanks to my grandmother's tuition, I can do that.'

'That's a relief. I thought I might have to live on cottage cheese and oranges.'

If he had been trying to induce a softer attitude with his sly reference to what had been her diet so long ago he failed. She said wearily, 'Look, I'm aware that you are capable of being very civilised and sophisticated about this. I'm still trying to adjust. Let's just pretend that we've met for the first time, shall we? It might be easier.'

'I doubt it,' he told her calmly, and at her questioning glance elaborated, 'If this was the first time we had met I'd be calculating how soon I could get you to bed. And I doubt if that's what you have in mind.'

It was years since she had blushed at a sexual innuendo. Yet she did it now, hating the shaming colour which flooded through her skin. Stiffly, her face averted, she retorted, 'In that you are totally correct. Pour yourself a drink in the sitting-room. I think today's newspaper is there. I'll be back shortly.'

There was little to do in the kitchen as the casserole was simmering away quietly in the oven and it was too early for her to prepare the salad she intended to have with it, but she pulled the vegetables out of the crisper and washed them, using the activity to stop herself from thinking.

An impossible endeavour. And it took her only a brief moment to realise that her main emotion was a desire to watch Jeff Caldwell and Brett March choke on their lies.

Not, she admitted with reluctant fairness, that they could be blamed for the whole fiasco. If she had not succumbed to the violence of her own desires she might have been able to convince Ryan that she was not the tough little amoralist he thought her. But even that would not have made much difference. She remembered the night he had looked at Elizabeth and fallen in love with her, a cynic caught by innocence. Venetia had had no counter to that kind of overwhelming emotion.

Well, it was all in the past. She could look back on the Venetia Gamble who had felt the keen bite of betrayal with a kind of pity not unmixed with sadness. She had thought herself so independent, so self-sufficient, but at heart she had been a romantic idiot, glorifying an ordinary affair with the attributes of a grand passion; she knew better now.

'What do you want to drink?'

Startled, she looked up. Ryan was in the doorway, his expression quizzical. 'Oh, gin and tonic, please. Very weak.'

He had it ready for her when she came back into the sitting-room. It was just as she liked it and she thanked him and sat down, wondering rather defiantly just how one behaved in such an extraordinary situation.

At the back of her mind was the niggling fact that he had definitely not reacted to John's existence in the way she would have expected. She would have felt more confident if he had shown anger and outrage at her behaviour.

He looked about the room before commenting idly, 'You've made no changes to the place. You don't really live here, do you? You're still a visitor in your grandmother's house.'

She took a small sip of her drink. 'I suppose that's how it appears, but I see no reason to alter an already pleasant house.'

'You're a transient, Venetia. You have no ties here now that your grandmother is dead. As your book is set in New Zealand it would make it much easier if we worked on it there.'

'There's nothing to stop you from going back,' she said indifferently. 'I'm happy here.'

He smiled and she could see that he was not going to give up. A cold chill in the region of her stomach felt suspicously like fear. She knew just how persistent Ryan could be, using a lethal combination of charm, determination and ruthlessness to attain his ends.

He began to talk of a political scandal which had recently erupted in New Zealand; as always, he was immensely interesting, the sheer entertainment of his story almost obscuring the keen, clever mind behind the words. Insensibly, in spite of the fact that she knew what he was doing, Venetia relaxed. The drink slid smoothly down her throat and she listened and nodded and made comments, enjoying herself as she had not for a long time.

'You have an extremely good brain,' he said after some time. That disciplined mouth hardened and his eyes narrowed for a second. 'Do you miss working?'

'No. I work, and it's a job I enjoy doing.'

He nodded, watching her with half-closed eyes. 'Now, perhaps. How was it before John was born? You should have told me, Venetia. At the very least I would have supported you.'

There was a note in his voice she didn't understand. She said crisply, 'My grandmother was not a poor woman, Ryan. She was quite happy to see that I didn't starve.'

'I find it angers me that my child was cared for by others.'

She shrugged. 'It does your character honour, but John was conceived the last time we were—together. It was not your fault.'

'I thought that you were protected.'

'I was on the pill, but I'd had ty—a tummy bug while I was away, and that had upset the cycle. It was just unfortunate.'

'*What* did you have?' And when she remained silent he said quietly, 'Typhoid.' And swore.

She shrugged. 'What does that matter? People who go poking their noses into other people's disasters can expect to pick up other people's diseases. I was lucky. I'd been working at the hospital and they knew what it was. Plenty died, including one who should have had the medicines I used.'

Incredibly he was white under his tan. He said on an impeded note, 'So when you came back—you'd just recovered from typhoid. And I hit you with the fact that our affair was over. And I——'

Venetia was not vindictive. Even in the depths of her pain and anger she had never wanted him hurting. She said quickly, 'As for the end of the affair, I already knew. You and Elizabeth took one look at each other and I saw that that was all that was necessary. I don't blame you— I never did. Falling in love is not anything you have any control over. It wasn't as though you had ever lied to me. Everything that happened was just as much my fault as yours.'

Harshly he retorted, 'Was that why you didn't tell me? Because you felt some kind of self-flagellating guilt? I'd thought you a clearer thinker than that, Venetia. You must have known that I would accept him, that I'd have married you. In the circles we moved in I would have been the first to know if you had been unfaithful.'

'Unfaithfulness,' she pointed out acidly, 'is the prerogative of married couples.'

He drained the whisky in his glass and set the glass down in a sharp, jerky movement. His anger was very real, a palpable, dark emotion which trapped her in her chair. She sat very still, her wide eyes caught by the unusual abruptness of his movements. One of the things which pulled such a fierce physical response from her was the lazy grace he possessed, so at variance with the whiplash strength of his lean body. He was tall, but not massive; she had heard him described as elegant more than once and she had agreed, hugging to herself her knowledge of the magnificent strength hidden by that elegance.

Now he bent his gaze on her and said icily, 'It seems more than likely that you were indulging in a little revenge.'

'No doubt you're right.' Her voice came out as prim and sedate as that of a Victorian child, an impression immediately submerged by the delicate malice of her voice as she said, 'You know me so well.'

'I'm beginning to wonder if I ever knew you.'

They stared at each other across the tranquil room, the stares a challenge which had been long in the breeding.

Perhaps it was just as well that there was an interruption. John appeared in the doorway, flushed and fretful, and announced belligerently, 'I don't want to stay in bed now, I'm not sick any more. I want to watch television. Right now.'

'OK,' Venetia said peaceably. She got to her feet and took him with her into the room which held the set. He was radiant and a bit suspicious, but she turned the set on and tucked him into his beanbag, arranged the panda bear beside him and waited while he registered that it was time for the news.

'I hate this,' he said crossly.

'Sorry, that's all that's on.'

He stared accusingly at her. 'I don't want to see it.'

She nodded. 'I don't blame you. Boring, isn't it? Would you rather have that ice-cream I promised you?'

He struggled free of the clutches of the beanbag and said vigorously, 'Yes, please. Is it mango and peach?'

'It is, my darling.'

He relaxed and took her hand, all belligerence gone. 'OK,' he said charmingly.

He ate it at the kitchen table, seeming not to notice that Ryan had come in, although both adults could hardly miss the sideways looks he kept stealing at this tall intruder.

When he had finished he drank a glass of orange juice and yawned and made no protest when Venetia said briskly, 'Back to bed now.'

He did object, however, when she went to pick him up. 'I'm big now,' he told her indignantly. 'You just remember that. I don't have to be carried like a baby.'

Downstairs, after she had tucked him in again, she met the hooded irony of Ryan's gaze with a hint of defiance. He said only, however, 'I see you've learned to manage him.'

'He has,' she said judicially, 'the stubbornness of a pig, and a temper to match.'

'Pigs have bad tempers?'

Her laughter was sudden, rich and warm. 'Try to take one of her piglets away from a sow and see.'

'I wonder where he got it from,' he mused with wry humour.

She grinned. 'I wonder. In my grandmother's idiom, he can be led but not driven. Actually, I doubt if the leading will be possible for much longer. Fortunately he's the sort of child you can reason with. Sometimes you have to wait for the tantrum to subside before he'll listen to the reasoning, but usually it works.'

'I think I'm going to like him,' he said slowly, as if he was surprised by the realisation.

She gave him a twisted smile. 'I hope so. He's very like you.'

'That,' he said sombrely and deliberately, 'is probably the strongest reason for me to *dis*like him.'

CHAPTER SIX

MUCH later, as she readied herself for bed, Venetia wondered just what that last comment meant. The Ryan she remembered had been totally assured, so confident in his own integrity that he would never have admitted to qualms.

Guiltily she realised that she was far too absorbed in him. She would have to forget those weeks when they were lovers and her life had been a rich material in all the colours of passion; it might help to remember the aftermath, when for months she had thought that death would be preferable to the dark night of the soul she had endured.

In spite of the tension that gripped her she managed to sleep, to wake to an overcast morning and a John who had developed more spots during the night and was busy trying to count them.

He lifted a rosy, cross face to Venetia as she came through the door and stopped wriggling long enough to pant, 'I can't see my back. I've got fifty-two on my tummy.'

Fifty-two was a number he was particularly fond of. Venetia smiled. 'Shall I count the ones on your back?'

'No! I want to do it myself.'

'Well, try Pandy. He might be able to see them.'

He was quite happy to follow her suggestion, and came padding downstairs a few minutes later to inform her that he had fifty-two spots on his back, too.

'Have you, indeed?' she said cheerfully, giving the coffee-pot a thoughtful look. There had been no sign of Ryan and he had always been an early riser, but she was not going looking for him. He could, she thought crisply, fall in with her routine or cook his own meals.

'I'd better put some lotion on you,' she told her son. 'Are they itchy?'

'Pandy says they are itchy, itchy, itchy, but I'm not scratching mine,' he told her righteously. 'Pandy scratches his.'

'Oh, wicked Pandy. He's going to be covered with scars. Come on, let's see to them.'

Duly anointed he ate his usual breakfast, chattering cheerfully as he did so. He had no sign of a temperature and was obviously not going to stay in bed any longer than it took for the novelty to wear off. He did not mention Ryan until the back door opened and he came in, hot and sweating after a run.

Then John demanded loudly, 'Why is that man still here?'

Oh lord, Venetia thought. Stupidly, she hadn't anticipated jealousy.

She opened her mouth to make some soothing reply, but Ryan forestalled her. 'Because I'm your father,' he said, his expression daring Venetia to deny it.

John's eyes rounded in surprise, then the lashes drooped in a way very familiar to Venetia. He firmed his mouth before asking stubbornly, 'Why don't you live with us then, like Jamie's daddy?'

'Because I didn't know where you lived,' Ryan said. 'As soon as I did I came.'

To Venetia's surprise John accepted this. 'Are you going to live with us all the time now?' he demanded.

Ryan's eyes met Venetia's. She saw the mockery brilliant in them as he said, 'I don't know. We'll just have to see how things work out. But I won't ever forget you, even if we do live in different houses. You'll be seeing a lot of me from now on.' He turned and said over his shoulder, 'Give me time to have a shower and I'll be down.'

There was silence for a while after he had left. John ate his way through a piece of toast with honey on it then stated with relish, 'Pandy says his father lives in Africa and is never coming home.'

'Poor Pandy,' Venetia said consolingly. 'Never mind, he has you to look after him.'

This put a new complexion on things. He spent some moments with his head tilted to one side while he considered it, then nodded and climbed down from the table. 'I'm sick,' he told her. 'Pandy and me are going back to bed. We want you to come and tuck us up.'

He was going to be more demanding than normal, but it seemed that Ryan's blunt way of breaking the news had been as easy on the child's psyche as any more graduated method could have been.

When she came back down Ryan was in the kitchen drinking coffee. Above the rim of the mug his eyes were speculative. Venetia sent him a faint smile.

'Well?'

Her shoulders lifted. 'He seems quite cheerful about it, although I'm afraid Pandy's father is not coming home.'

After she had explained Ryan looked thoughtful and said, 'I imagine a certain amount of jealousy is inevitable.'

'Yes, I suppose so. He'll get over it. He's possessive, but not normally jealous.'

'You know him better than I.'

She opened her mouth to say something, but he forestalled her with a simple statement. 'A state of affairs I intend to rectify.'

Her eyes met and held his. She felt the corners of her mouth tighten at the arrogant certitude she read there, but all she said was, 'What would you like to eat?'

He shrugged. 'I can get it. Aren't you keen to start work?'

'Well, yes, but——'

'One of the consequences of having a mother who was too wrapped up in her own life to cope with the normal parental role is a fair competence in the kitchen,' he said coolly. 'I'm quite capable of getting my own breakfast.'

She smiled far too sweetly. 'Good. How about using a dishwasher?'

'That, too.'

'Be my guest.'

In the study she stood for a moment surveying the room with unseeing eyes. What exactly did she feel for him now? A vast caution; she had no intention of falling in love with him again. The last time had been so traumatic that it had scarred her for life.

But oh, he excited her; she felt more alive now than she had in the almost six years since their parting. Somehow he made it possible for her to function on a level which was far beyond the normal; he stimulated her brain and her senses, so that she saw more clearly, was open to a wider range of input. Perhaps she was an adrenalin junkie, fixated on him because he was the source of her 'high'.

Whatever it was, she did not love him. She could not love him. He had shown only too clearly that he wanted a sweet, docile wife, one who put him before all else.

Unfortunately, she decided as she moved purposefully over to her desk and unlocked the drawer which held her manuscript, she was not able to give anyone that kind of uncritical, selfless devotion. Her work was necessary to her. It always would be.

She worked with the total absorption she had trained in herself, concentrating so fiercely that she did not hear John's entrance until he was almost at her knee.

'Yes?' she said vaguely, lifting her head to stare at him.

He was, she realised blankly, extremely indignant, his features flushed and belligerent.

'You tell him to go away,' he ordered. 'He's not my daddy. My daddy is nice.'

Venetia blinked once or twice. 'What's the matter?'

'I want to watch television and that man said to me that I can't. You tell him that I can so.' He stared boldly at her as he added the clincher. 'I'm sick, the doctor said so!'

Venetia looked sternly at him. 'You know perfectly well that there is nothing on television at this hour of the morning for you to watch! And as for being sick, my boy, sick boys stay in bed and sleep a lot and feel awful. Are you in bed?'

He grinned. 'No.'

'Are you asleep?'

A wider grin. 'No.'

Venetia leaned over the desk and fixed him with a stern eye. 'Are you feeling awful?'

He looked up at her through his lashes. 'I'm a little bit itchy,' he offered. 'Pandy is sick.'

'Then Pandy had better go up to bed and read a couple of books and do some colouring in and drink some lemonade and have a little snooze.' A slight movement across the room caught Venetia's attention. Ignoring it she finished firmly, 'And when Pandy is feeling better and if he is going to behave himself, we can let him have a go at his computer. Now, off you go.'

John hesitated, his fingers working in the soft toy's fur. He looked suddenly anxious as he asked, 'Is he really my daddy?'

'Yes.'

He nodded, his dark eyes trustful but worried. 'Will I like him?'

Venetia risked a glance at the door and saw Ryan there, still as a statue, his expression bleak yet determined.

'Yes,' she said firmly. 'It might take a little time because he isn't used to having a little boy and you aren't used to having a father, but he loves you very much and you will love him too.'

'OK,' he sighed, apparently not at all thrilled by this information. Venetia sighed a little too, but she waited until he was out of sight. Ryan had soundlessly left the doorway before she had finished speaking, presumably to leave the way clear.

She sat frowning for a few minutes, staring absently at the keyboard. From a distance she heard John's voice; it sounded quite cheerful, but then he could have been having one of his interminable conversations with his bear.

Jealousy, she thought drearily, had to be one of the bitterest human emotions, and one of the most difficult to deal with. Poor John.

She got up and went out into the passage, looking towards the sound of his voice. It came from the kitchen and yes, Ryan's deep tones came in answer. Feeling suddenly desolate, she went back into the study and sat down, but it was some time before she started work again, and when she did it was difficult to keep her mind active on the subject of grammatical errors and mistakes.

By lunch time she was pleased to see the amount of work she had got through; another two days and the manuscript would be ready to post to the publisher. It wasn't, she thought critically, bad, although as always she was disappointed at the difference between her initial vision and the final result.

Ryan had found the materials for a salad with cold meat, and with John's help had set the table. They appeared to be on quite amiable terms now, which was a relief. She washed her hands and came into the kitchen with a determined smile.

It was an oddly pleasant meal, in spite of the tense undercurrents. John ate largely as he always did, but said little, although his glance lingered frequently on the chiselled features of his father. Ryan met his eyes directly, smiling; Venetia noted with resignation that the charm worked as potently on small boys as it did on impressionable women. Half-way through the meal he asked about her morning's work with an interest which didn't seem feigned.

'Oh, well, this is the boring bit,' she replied, and surprised herself by telling him of her subtle disappointment in each work.

'I can understand that,' he said. 'We dream of perfection, we plan it, but the result is always a long way short.' A cynical smile sharpened his angular features. 'That's life.'

She wondered just how life had failed to live up to Ryan's hopes. He had always seemed so much in control of his life, dominating it with an effortless ease which made you forget that he was only mortal. It had to be Elizabeth's death. He must have loved her very much. And she felt again the pain of that old jealousy, mixed with the aching loss she had never been able to free herself from.

Stupid, because how could he help falling in love? How could anyone resist that passionate yearning for the other half? Most of the best poetry and much of the greatest literature in the world would never have been written if love was easily avoided. Once, aeons ago, she had questioned the existence of love; she knew better now.

After lunch John toted the bear up the stairs and into his bedroom, humming the little tune which accompanied his sense of well-being. Venetia drained her coffee and said, 'I'll work until John decides to emerge. Are you OK?'

'I can manage to amuse myself,' he returned drily. 'Leave the dishes, I'll put them into the dishwasher.'

'Thank you.' She knew she sounded stilted, but there was no need for him to look at her with that narrow, taunting smile.

Thank heavens for her work! At least while she was concentrating she wasn't able to fret and worry over his presence, or his plans.

John's waking coincided with the arrival of Kay Dodwell, Jamie clutching her hand. They followed Ryan into the kitchen where John was happily eating a large orange, and it took only one look for Venetia to see that Kay, always astute, had recognised Ryan. She introduced them, noted, again with resignation, Kay's stunned reaction to Ryan's virile brand of charm, and peeled and quartered another orange for Jamie.

'This,' John announced with an elaborate insouciance, 'is my daddy. He's bigger than yours.'

Jamie eyed Ryan interestedly. ''My daddy's got a bigger tummy.'

'Alas,' mourned Kay, subduing her laughter by a rigorous effort of will, 'he is so right.'

Venetia grinned, mischief dancing in her face, but all she said was, 'You boys eat your oranges, and then you can get the blocks and the truck and the bulldozer out and play with them. Kay, would you like a cup of coffee?'

'I'd love one.'

If Ryan had any sense of decency he would have left the two of them alone. But no, he stayed, using his potent mixture of charm and intelligence and arrogance to conquer Kay. Venetia fumed silently even as she appreciated his wit and style, and Kay's unselfconscious appreciation only served to add to her anger. He should not, she thought in disgruntlement all the stronger for being quite unreasonable, be so damned attractive! Or so pleasant. He should not even be there!

'And how is John behaving?' Kay asked cheerfully. 'He's such a possessive little soul, I imagine you're having to tread fairly warily. He's not used to sharing Venetia's attention.'

'Only with her work,' Ryan commented with smooth insolence, watching from beneath his lashes as angry colour flooded Venetia's cheeks.

Intelligent, perceptive Kay said promptly, 'All children are accustomed to sharing their mother with her work, whatever that happens to be. My talents are purely domestic, but I concentrate just as much on my activities as Venetia does on hers. You can get lost to the world trying to fathom out a knitting pattern. It's no longer fashionable to sneer at women who choose to remain at home, you know.'

Ryan's grin slashed across his face. 'That was the furthest thing from my mind, but your point is taken,' he said blandly. 'And yes, I note a certain amount of resentment on John's part. He will, however, get used to sharing his mother's day with me.'

Kay looked from Ryan's challenging face to the smooth, cool mask of Venetia's, and said a little too brightly, 'Well, that's a good thing. He spends a lot of time with us, and James is always ready to be a surrogate father, but John needs his own. That was a wickedly gleeful look he gave poor old Jamie when he boasted of your height!'

They all smiled, and looked across the room to where both boys were occupied in the never-ending task of building fortifications and roadworks only to knock them down and start again. John was standing up, explaining something if his large gestures were any indication; Jamie crouched a little way away, listening and nodding.

'There you have it,' Kay said cheerfully. 'John leads, Jamie follows.'

John looked up and with a possessive look of determination ran across to his mother and leant against her knee, watching Ryan from beneath his lashes. He couldn't have been more explicit if he had shouted his determination to keep his mother for himself. With a wry, affectionate look Venetia felt his forehead. It was cool, although she noticed that a couple of new spots had emerged on his cheeks.

'May we have a drink of lime juice?' he asked politely.

'Yes, I'll get one, and then you and Jamie can watch *Play School*. How would you like that?'

Kay got to her feet and took her son's hand. 'Lovely, except that Jamie and I have to go home. I have dinner to put on and then I have to ferry Sarah to gymnastics. Say goodbye, Jamie.'

Later that night something Kay had said surfaced in an entirely unexpected way. John was sound asleep and Ryan had searched through the record cabinet before putting on a piano quartet by Fauré. The subtle, inventive music was oddly comforting; Venetia listened to the lyrical notes flow past and let her mind go with them. Just once she thought that this was how it should have been, the two of them sharing an experience with no need for words, their son lying asleep in his room upstairs. Dreams, she chided herself ironically, they caused more trouble than outright malice.

When the record was over Ryan opened his eyes, catching her looking at him, and demanded without preamble, 'Why did your friend say that her husband liked being a surrogate father? Do you dump John on them?'

The bitter attack caught her unawares. She lifted her chin before answering quietly, 'Jamie and John are very good friends. They spend most of their time with each other, about half the time here, the other half at Kay's. As Kay is very happily married, her husband is on the scene quite a bit.' She hesitated, wondering if she was being foolish but added anyway, 'I thought it was important for John to have a man somewhere in his life.'

'Someone more stable than your lovers?'

She replied ironically, 'My grandmother had very modern attitudes in many ways, but she did not approve of promiscuity. And as I didn't think it was fair to leave her to babysit, I haven't exactly lived a life of riotous social whirling.'

He leaned back in the chair he had made his own and surveyed her enigmatically, brows raised. When he spoke his voice was almost offhand. 'Are you trying to tell me that there have been no lovers?'

Some small whisper of caution at the back of her mind insinuated itself through the longing that was tugging at her body. It could be dangerous to admit the lack of masculine interest in her life. Holding his gaze she said just as deliberately, 'I'm not trying to tell you anything, Ryan. You have no rights where I'm concerned, certainly no right to take a prurient interest in my emotional life.'

Yes, that stung. His heavy lids drooped even lower until all she could see were gleaming spears of obsidian, sharply penetrating. 'John is my son and you have been responsible for his well-being. That gives me a vested interest in all aspects of your life, wouldn't you say?'

'Perhaps.' She registered his surprise with a slight quirk of the muscles beside her mouth. 'But I'm afraid I'm not going to tell you whether or not I have lovers.'

'If your response yesterday was any indication,' he pointed out offensively, 'you've been celibate for a while. I know frustration when I see it. You were wild for a man. Any man.'

The insult set fire to her temper; she could feel blind, black rage shooting out of the top of her head so violently that she trembled with it. 'You smug, insufferable swine! How dare you come here, with your crude innuendoes and snide insults! What gives you the right to judge me? Tell me, how many women have you slept with? Can you count them? Can you even remember them? I know exactly how many men I've made love with, each and every one, and I can recall them——'

He lunged out of the chair and hauled her to her feet by the upper arms, his face so taut with rage that she fell silent even before he shook her into stillness. Through clenched teeth he muttered, 'Shut up, damn you, shut up! You're screaming like a fishwife. I don't want to hear about your lovers, you fill me with disgust when you boast of them...'

'Ryan, let me go,' she whispered, afraid of the explosion she had set off. His eyes were black as hell, yet there was fire in them, a dark, obscuring flame that answered the violent uprush of emotion in her. 'Ryan,' she repeated almost imploringly.

His hands tightened on her arms, foiling her attempt to pull away. She stared into his face, grabbing desperately for the strength of will to stop this before it started, but his mouth took hers and all caution, all sense, vanished in the incredible hunger which shook through her.

She went under as if drowning, opening her mouth to his savage invasion, welcoming the pain that was not pain because it came from every pleasure centre in her body, swift and searing as an electric shock, leaping from nerve to nerve until she was deaf and blind and dumb, all of her attention fixed on her other senses.

Like scent. He smelled so good, of warm, aroused male. And taste. On his probing tongue, in his mouth, lingered the faint essence of the wine they had had for dinner, but mostly her mouth accepted his own special flavour, potent, exciting, more precious than the best vintage champagne. And the feel of him, the hard, powerful muscles so pleasurably contrasted with the smooth, flowing silk of the skin over them, a magnificent masculine dichotomy which conquered all that was feminine in her.

And through it all that profound sense of recognition, the instinctual knowledge that from among all the men in the world this man was her mate.

He lifted his head a fraction and muttered something; the words came erotically against her lips, the soft movements firing her blood anew. She made a strange sound in the back of her throat and kissed the corner of his mouth, the stubborn line of chin and jaw, the beautiful strong length of his neck.

He said through clenched teeth, 'Oh, God, why can't I control this? Why does it have to be you?'

The torment in the words chilled her blood. She looked up and her hands came swiftly up to frame his face. He had kissed her so hard that her mouth was bruised; it surprised her to see that his lips, too, were slightly swollen. But it was the bitter anguish in his eyes which made her say softly, 'Don't, Ryan. Don't my dear. It's not like that.'

He closed his eyes and buried his proud face in her throat. She felt his mouth move but he said nothing, made no sound, and after a moment he lifted his head and looked down at her, all traces of torment gone. His face was a smooth, polished mask, impersonal, chiselled with desire. He looked as though he had fought a battle with himself and won, at great, almost unbearable cost.

Venetia was frightened. She made to step back but he said beneath his breath, 'No, no you don't. Let's see if all my memories have been highly coloured figments of my imagination, shall we? Nothing could be as good as I remember it.'

Slowly, in pain as great as his, she said, 'I don't think this is a good idea. We'd better stop.'

'Just as it's getting interesting?' He touched the pulse in her throat then smiled, his eyes narrow and dangerous. 'Don't you want to remember, Venetia?'

Really frightened now, she fought to free herself from the hunger and the longing and the fierce bondage of her body, and said sharply, 'No! This has gone far enough. You don't want to make love, you want to punish me.'

'You always were too quick for your own good, but you're not quite there. It's not so much you I want to punish as myself.'

Appalled, she flinched away from the brand of his mouth on her shoulder. Self-preservation warred with the heated tide of sensation; she felt the sting of his kisses as he sought remembered hollows that were particularly sensitive, and at his touch desire swept through her in spite of the cruel finesse he was using as a weapon.

She knew what he wanted to do. He had conquered his own demons, the lack of control which bedevilled him so, and now he was going to force her into the wildly ungovernable region of the senses which she remembered so well, and he was going to stay fully in command of himself while he did it.

Shudders ran through her, and she cried, 'No!'

'Hush,' he whispered. 'Hush.'

But she pushed at him, trying to get away until he lost his temper and collapsed backwards on to the sofa, landing beneath her. Before she had time to make her escape, he yanked the dress she was wearing over her head and she was lying on top of him in the camisole and half-slip and little bikini pants which were all she had on under it.

A dark flush crawled along his cheekbones. He fixed her with a blind stare and opened his mouth on the shadowed nipple beneath the pale, thin fabric. She gasped, transfixed by a pang of sensation so poignant that she was lost, her small body flowing like silk over his as his mouth worked on her flesh. Her fingers tore at the buttons of his shirt, slid over skin as hot as fire, spread with luxurious, wanton delight over the unyielding wall of his chest.

She groaned and he moved his magical mouth away. 'Look,' he said thickly. 'See what I can do to you, Venetia.'

Almost beside herself with desire she followed his gaze to where the wet material of the chemise clung. He buried his face between her breasts and moved it slightly from side to side, pulling at the cloth so that it tantalised the sensitive nipples into fiery points of desire, and asked huskily, 'Did you feed John yourself?'

'Yes, for seven months.' The words were heavy, almost without tone or meaning. She fought a wave of passion so intense that she ached with it, and without volition her hips moved and thrust, searching in the most primitive way for satisfaction of the fire he had kindled in her.

He was like rock beneath her, rigid with restraint, but she felt the signs of his body's arousal and moved again, desperate to assuage that ache.

At that moment there was nothing she wanted more than what was going to happen; the happy, productive years slid away into a kind of grey limbo, all her calm logic dissipated like smoke in the wind and she was lost, abandoned to desire, greedy for love and the heady fulfilment that would follow, impatient to appease that inner knowledge that for her he was the only man.

She smiled, a heavy-lidded, enigmatic sphinx's smile, and watched as his mouth fastened once more on to her breast. How could it be so different, she thought dazedly, a child...

Her body convulsed in an agony of pleasure. 'Gently,' Ryan whispered. 'I want to take hours... It's been so long that I want to savour every minute, every sweet second...'

But the fiery tide of passion had been reft by reason. John, she thought, struggling to remember something. Oh, God, *John*!

Aloud, her voice heavy and laboured, she choked, 'No! I don't want to get pregnant again!'

CHAPTER SEVEN

RYAN stiffened, then released her from the heated prison of his mouth. For a long moment he lay with his face buried in her breasts, until he looked up in bitter denial.

'Is it possible?'

Venetia nodded, her wild eyes revealing blatantly what this was doing to her. 'Yes, it is. I don't—I'm not——'

He said something which might have shocked her if she hadn't felt exactly the same. The flush of passion faded, to be replaced by frustration and a devouring hunger which was an exact counterpart of the emotions eating through Venetia.

His arms tightened across her hips, forcing her into intimate and fierce contact with him, and in spite of the resurgence of common sense which had come so late and so painfully, she moved against him, holding him cradled for a second against her.

Then he pushed her away, saying in a harsh, goaded voice, 'For God's sake, get your dress on.'

She got to her feet, shivering now with reaction and a hunger so fierce she thought it might eat through her bones. For the first time with him she had managed to follow the dictates of her head, she had not surrendered to her body's needs. She should be feeling strong and brave and mature. Instead she could only wish that she had never remembered John, never thought for that second of her unprotected state.

For some seconds she stood gazing around her in bewilderment. Shame kept her eyes averted from the man who lay on the sofa. She saw her dress in a heap almost across the room and went quickly towards it.

From behind came Ryan's voice, cynical, as hard as the words he spoke. 'You could earn yourself a mint of money for a photograph of you now. Titillation personified; sex in its most dangerous guise.'

Her colour left her. As she yanked the dress over her head she knew what he had seen. The half-slip had gone, and above the scrap of her bikini panties the chemise clung softly, lovingly, to breasts which showed only too plainly her arousal.

She swung around, her expression almost pleading. 'Ryan, can't you see that this won't work? I——'

He was still stretched out, the lean, powerful length of him at ease in spite of his watchful eyes. 'I don't know, darling,' he drawled. 'A man would be a fool to pass up what you are offering.'

She exploded. 'I'm not *offering* anything, you bastard! How dare you come here and think you've got the right to take up where you left off, as if I were a woman you've bought! You walked out on me, you didn't want what I offered you then, I'm damned if I'm going to make the same mistake again!'

'You want me,' he said coolly.

She clenched her teeth, spitting hot words through them. 'As you once said to me on one of the more memorable occasions of my life, you'll probably always be able to make me want you. It didn't mean a thing to you then, it doesn't mean a thing to me now.'

The light was golden over his face, but it revealed nothing. Even his eyes were blank, hooded and controlled. 'I lied,' he said flatly. 'Oh, I thought I was telling the truth, I'd convinced myself that what I felt for you was lust, pure and simple, and because I have a strong Puritan streak I hurt you, just as you're trying to hurt me now.'

'I suppose you're going to try to convince me that you loved me,' she sneered, holding fast to her anger because she couldn't weaken, she had to defend herself against him and this merciless power he possessed over her. 'Amazing the lengths you'll go to to get a woman into bed with you!'

His expression hardened. 'No, I'm not going to try to convince you of anything, you wouldn't believe a word I said anyway. Quite frankly, I can't say I blame you. But——'

Alarmed, she stepped back as he got up lithely from the sofa and came towards her, tall and almost menacing in her grandmother's pretty room. 'This,' he said softly, putting out a hand to touch the pulse which beat its betraying little message at the base of her throat, 'is something that neither of us can ignore in the hope that it will go away. You may resent it, I certainly do, but it exists, and the last six years don't seem to have made any difference.'

Her breath was trapped in her throat, beneath the caressing stroke of his fingertips. Carefully she said, 'That's why you shouldn't be here, Ryan.'

His fingers smoothed upwards to curl around her small jaw. He was smiling, those hard eyes gittering as he said calmly, 'On the contrary. If I've learned anything in these six years it's that running away is useless. That's why if you don't want any more children, my temptress, you had better get off to your doctor tomorrow. I'll give you a week. Then I'm going to sate myself in you until both of us are too exhausted to get out of bed.'

Her blood ran cold. She tried to jerk her head away, but his long fingers tightened just short of cruelty. 'You can't be serious,' she protested.

'Never more. One way or another I'm going to rid myself of the weakness you represent. I've never had anything but contempt for men—or women—who are slaves of their passions. I don't intend to be one. Abstinence doesn't seem to have conquered this need I have, so we'll see how a depraved indulgence works. I imagine that after a few months of taking you I'll be sickened by a surfeit of that delectable little body, and then perhaps you and I can work out some sort of existence which will supply John with the stable life he needs and deserves.'

He did not say it, but she knew that he envisaged a life when that inconvenient, overwhelming passion would finally be appeased, and exorcised, and she would no longer bother him. And she was angry and terrified, because for her that would never happen. If he died she would perhaps be able to love someone else, but it would never be like this. Never this violent, all-consuming sweetness in the blood, this communion of body and spirit and mind. What he saw as a weakness to be cut out of his life she knew to be love.

And if she allowed him to take her it would destroy her.

'I won't allow you to treat me as if I was an illness you can be vaccinated against,' she said with an icy composure which hid her fear and despair.

That maddening, frightening smile still clung to the finely cut contours of his mouth. It didn't reach his eyes, which were determined and a little speculative. There was fire in the dark depths, but it was not the sort which warmed; it was the fire imprisoned in the heart of ice.

'You won't be able to stop me,' he said quietly, not bothering to mute the threat. 'Because we both know that I only have to kiss you and I could take you on the kitchen table if I wanted to. And I do want to. When the day comes that I can look at you dispassionately without this bloody clenching in my loins, I'll walk out the door and you only ever need see me again in relation to John.'

The hand on her chin loosened, moving up to sweep gently along her mouth in a stroke as light as it was tantalising. Every need denied to her hungry body came scorching back to life; she shivered and stepped away and said stonily, 'I'm not going to be your sexual slave. You forget, I've already been there and I didn't much like it. If you want sex on tap you're going to have to marry me.'

The last observation was flung into the silence with a reckless disregard for prudence. She didn't mean it, would not marry him, but she wanted to tilt him off balance, make him lose that control he was so proud of.

Instead, he merely looked quizzically at her, his mouth quirking as though she had just supplied him with an answer he had long sought.

Suddenly she was exhausted. Her shoulders stayed gallantly erect, but her voice was defeated as she turned away from the hard derision in his gaze. 'That was a stupid thing to say, because I wouldn't marry you. I'm going to bed, Ryan, I'm tired.'

He let her go, following her within a few minutes. In her lonely bedroom she waited until she heard the soft, prowling footsteps come up the stairs and along the passage to the bathroom, then she forced herself into her nightgown and climbed into bed, to lie tense and aching for what seemed to be hours.

She had just got off to sleep when a wail from John brought her to her feet. Without bothering to put on a dressing-gown she ran quickly to his room. He was sitting bolt upright in the bed, tears trickling down his cheeks, his mouth open in a roar of distress.

The brilliance of the lamp made him flinch and glare at her, but the terror in his expression faded as the light began to banish the nightmare. Venetia came across the room and sat down beside him, drawing him into her arms.

'What was it?' she asked gently.

He shook his head violently and buried his pale little face in her shoulder.

'Darling, was it a bad dream?'

He sniffed, but his head jerked in affirmation.

'Never mind, I know how scary they are, but it was just a dream, lovey, it wasn't real.'

His sturdy body was tense and rigid. Clutching her he wriggled into her lap.

'Would you like a drink of lime juice?'

A violent shake of his head put paid to that idea.

'Sometimes it helps if you can talk about it,' she suggested. 'Shall we pretend it was a movie, and you can tell me what happened?'

Some of the tautness seemed to ease from his body, but after a moment's consideration he turned his head sideways and said, 'No, Mummy, you would be scared too.'

Love flowed through her body. He was so small, so valiant. It had to be an inbuilt instinct, she thought, this masculine urge to protect. Resting her cheek on his damp hair, she said tentatively, 'Pandy, then. Would he be frightened?'

He gulped and whispered, 'Pandy was there and he was scared—he——'

Venetia hugged him hard and began to rock him back and forth. 'Darling, it wasn't true, it was just a dream. See, I'm here, you're here, in your bedroom at home. Pandy's here too.'

'And I'm here,' Ryan said from the door.

John went very still. Quickly Venetia finished, 'And Daddy is here. Daddy is a big strong man, John, he wouldn't be frightened if you told him your dream.'

The firm little body relaxed. A wary eye peeked forth. With a caution that must have hurt Ryan, now standing by the bed, John asked, 'Can you kill monsters?'

'Everyone can kill monsters,' Ryan promised. 'Even monsters in dreams. You just have to know how.'

John emerged a little further from his refuge. He whispered, 'All right, I'll tell you. I want you to stay, Mummy, but don't you listen.'

'Hey, what gave you the idea that I can't kill monsters too?' she asked a little teasingly. 'I'll have you know that no monsters dare come into my dreams, they know they'll get chased right out again.'

He wrinkled his brow at that, but decided to accept it, thereby proving, Venetia thought fondly, that while chauvinism might be inherent in the male it was capable of being modified.

She listened carefully to his nightmare, a rambling tale of monsters with big teeth, and the chase and eventual capture of Pandy. In a very short time John was almost free of the lingering miasma of horror, but whenever his voice trembled Ryan would ask him what he would do if he was making a movie of it, and after suggestions from both parents for altering the course of the dream, John was sitting upright, his eyes sparkling, describing with large gestures a particularly clever move on Pandy's part.

'I think that would frighten any monster off,' Ryan said cheerfully. 'One of these days I'll take you to the set of a movie that I'm making.'

This had to be explained, and Ryan clearly went up several notches in his son's estimation. Yawning but excited, John began a rambling summary of a film Venetia had taken him to, breaking off at last to rub his eyes.

'I think you can get off to sleep again now that you know what to do if your dream comes back,' Venetia proposed in her most soothing tone, pushing the hair back from his warm brow. 'I'll get you a drink first. Would you like the light left on?'

Hesitantly, after a quick glance at his father from beneath his lashes, he whispered, 'I think Pandy would for a little while.'

Ryan said nothing, but as Venetia left the room she saw him tuck the bear in beside his son with a smile which held affection and a certain wry understanding. Yes, John needed a father.

He drank most of the lime juice then smiled cheerfully at both of them before snuggling beneath the covers. 'Pandy's tired,' he explained.

Venetia was still smiling as she faced Ryan outside her door. He said evenly, 'I take it Pandy is his *alter ego*. I thought only lonely children had imaginary playmates.'

'Did you? Have an imaginary playmate?'

He blinked, as though she had shocked him. After a short, rather tense pause he returned, 'Yes, as it happens, I did. But I was a lonely child.'

'And an imaginative one. John doesn't spend all of his time at nursery school or playing with Jamie. When he needs a playmate he has Pandy. He's growing away from it now; in a few more months he'll no longer need it.'

He nodded, not looking at her. When he spoke it was just to say her name on an almost questioning tone. She looked enquiringly at him and he lifted his hand and touched her cheek. It was an oddly tentative, almost hesitant movement. Wide-eyed, she stood very still, her gaze never leaving his face. His beard was a dark shadow blurring only slightly the determined contours of his jaw; as she watched she saw a muscle flex there, the little movement strangely evocative of profound stress.

He looked at her with deep, astonished eyes and said, half-beneath his breath, 'God, of all——' Her bewilderment must have impinged because he stopped, his lips clamping over whatever he had been about to say. The hand curved around her cheek moved, touched her mouth and the fragile temple, then dropped. Slowly, he said, 'I'll see you in the morning.'

It was difficult to turn away and take the weary steps back into her chaste bedroom. After the bout of passion earlier in the evening she had thought that she would never be able to face him again, but with their son as an intermediary that first meeting had passed without any embarrassment at all.

And somehow that last quiet little incident outside John's room had drawn the sting from her memories. Although she might never know what he had been thinking she had seen in his expression a haunting tenderness which had delighted even as it astonished her. If she hadn't known him better she would have thought that he had just been struck by a realisation so great that even his quick, intelligent brain had been unable to deal with it.

As she drifted off into sleep her wayward mind recalled the lean, wide shoulders, lightly scrolled with hair that arrowed down to his belt. He was like a statue in bronze brought to warm, dangerously attractive life. He made her hungry and excited, he satisfied her eyes as he entrapped the responses of her body and stimulated her mind.

Her last thought was that he had known just how to deal with his son's nightmare.

John woke the next morning with a man-size chip on his shoulder which he took out on his mother, refusing to eat his breakfast, scowling ferociously at her when she scotched his demand to be taken to the zoo. He was, she realised as she saw him stealing looks at his father, rather sorry that he had allowed himself to be coaxed into opening up to him. He was very much on his dignity, a fact which Ryan appreciated. After one wry exchange of glances with Venetia he set himself to recovering the ground which had been lost. He did it well, adopting a casual throw-away approach which had the effect of luring John on.

Venetia was reminded of a master hunter stalking a small, suspicous animal. It might have amused her if she hadn't been rather frightened by this indication of how good a psychologist Ryan was.

At least he didn't make any more threats like those of last night. While she worked she was able to put all such memories to the back of her mind, but as soon as she switched off the word processor they came surging back. And with them the memory of what had happened after the nightmare. Not that Ryan had showed any signs of revealing what had led up to it.

All day he was pleasant, yet a little distant, talking after dinner about John with a calm reserve which paradoxically served to make her even more uneasy. When he was like this, his real emotions hidden behind a bland, uncommunicative front, he was at his most dangerous. She remembered the interview he had conducted with Periera, the dictator. Just so had he eased the man into relaxation before striking, using the telling phrase, the mild yet pointed comment to goad the man into revealing the brutal, vicious nature of his rule.

She couldn't rid herself of the dismaying suspicion that he was doing to her what he had done to Periera, what he was doing to John. A little coaxing, a little subterfuge, and then the sudden strike behind the barricades, and John would learn to love him; and she—well, he had spelled out what he intended for her.

Never, she thought bitterly. She had more pride.

During the week that followed she was wary and defensive, finding it difficult to cope with a Ryan who was uncannily pleasant, calm and easy to please, apparently devoting all his energies to building some sort of relationship with John. In spite of her suspicions Venetia slowly relaxed, became more at ease when the date he had given her passed and he made no attempt to make love to her.

Perhaps, she thought carefully, he had changed his mind. The thought brought such a pang of pain that she was revolted by her own duplicity. Had her subconscious been nurturing hopes?

For a couple of days after that she was stiff and uneasy with him, but although she read a dry mockery in his face he made no effort to persuade her, and in the delight she felt in his company she pushed her fears to the back of her mind.

John's spots flourished and faded. He began to accept Ryan as an inevitable part of his life. Venetia forcibly refrained from checking her manuscript one more time, parcelled it up and posted it off. That night Ryan took them both out to dinner at the local McDonald's, and

when a pleased John had been put to bed he opened a
bottle of champagne and poured it.

'And what,' she asked almost nervously, 'is this for?'

He looked amused, and brought her the glass of pale
wine. 'Stop looking at me as if you suspect the worst. I
think we should drink to the success of your novel, that's
all.'

'I'm not used to champagne,' she said, but she followed his lead and tasted the fresh, delicious stuff.

Leaning back into the chair, he watched her with an
impassive expression which made her extremely nervous. 'I suppose not. You haven't exactly had an easy six
years of it, have you?'

She hunched her shoulders. 'It hasn't been bad. John
has been a constant joy, and my grandmother was—well,
you had to know her to appreciate her.'

'She didn't like me,' he said calmly. 'I wondered why,
at the time, but I can't say I blame her. She must have
thought I was a complete cad.'

It was important to disabuse him of that impression.
'She didn't. Until you came that day she had no idea
who—who the father was.'

'I see.'

She bit her lip. 'I heard Liz's voice at the door and in
panic I made Gran promise not to tell. You didn't have
to spell things out to her, she was as sharp as a tack.'

'Well, at least it explains why she was so stiff with us
both. Elizabeth said that you had always been her
favourite. She said that you were very alike.'

'I'm not so tough,' she said wryly, hurting at the sound
of Elizabeth's name.

He drank some champagne and turned the glass in his
long fingers, staring down into the glowing liquid as if he
was mesmerised. 'Why didn't you tell me that you were
pregnant?'

'I didn't know at first. I thought the symptoms were
just reaction.' She was not prepared to enlarge on that

and hurried on, 'When I realised I was already in Australia with Gran. And you were engaged to Liz. It didn't seem a tactful time to announce that you were about to become a father.'

He said unemotionally, 'I would have accepted him, Venetia.'

She drank a little more. He repeated his last observation and she looked up and nodded. 'Yes, I know,' she said on a sigh. 'But there was Elizabeth. She wouldn't have liked it, and who could blame her?'

He looked down, as if Elizabeth's name hurt. After a moment or two he said, 'Yes, she'd have hated it. I wish you had told me, however.'

She said uncertainly, 'There's no need to feel such responsibility. That last time—you didn't want—I——'

'That last time,' he said silkily, 'the same as every other time, I wanted you with a desperation which overthrew all reason, all logic. Ever since childhood, when I learned how dangerous emotions could be, I'd prided myself on my control. Until I met you I'd been able to deal with my own sexuality with restraint and a certain amount of sophistication. You were such a danger to me because the rules no longer applied. You had only to smile and I was lost to everything but a passion so fiercely irresistible that I felt nothing else. I hated it because you made me less than the man I thought I was.'

'You still hate it,' she said wearily.

'So do you. But this time, Venetia, I intend to face it.'

She ignored the icy chills running the length of her spine. 'I know. By indulging it to the point of depravity, wasn't that how you put it? I, however——'

'Did I say that?' he interrupted, looking amused. 'See how badly you affect my normal good sense? No, I no longer think that an affair will do the trick. There's something forbidden, something exciting about an affair. I think you have the right idea. We should try the routine of marriage.'

Venetia said with harsh distinctness, 'I don't happen to find that very amusing.'

'Who's joking?'

She put the glass down on the table beside her chair and looked at him. There was nothing to be gauged from his expression; he had the clear-cut determination of a devil, ice-carved features in the warm glow of the lamp.

'I didn't mean it,' she said at last. 'As you know.'

He moved his head a little and in the soft light of the lamp the small smile which moved his lips seemed faintly sinister. 'I prefer to think it was a Freudian slip,' he replied, too gently.

If he loved her she would walk across the world to marry him; marriage for any other reason was unthinkable. In a voice made gravelly by tension she said, 'Sorry, you'll have to settle for unlimited access to John.'

'Marriage is the only way to provide me with that.' He, too, put down his glass as a prelude to getting to his feet.

As he came towards her she saw that smile again, and this time there was no doubt about its quality. He looked sinfully dangerous, his eyes gleaming with the wild recklessness against which logic and intelligence were no protection. Venetia shrank back into her chair, and he stopped, frowning.

The telephone shrilled a summons. She stared at him, and then across the room at the instrument as though she had never heard it before. Ryan gave a muffled curse and pulled her out of the chair, propelling her towards it with fingers which bit savagely into the slope of her shoulder.

It was her Uncle Bob, tired and obviously very worried, to tell her that her aunt was in hospital and asking for her.

'What's the matter with her?' she demanded, fear sharpening the words.

'The doctor isn't sure. Possibly her heart.'

Slumping into a chair she pushed a strand of silvery hair back from her cold cheek. 'All right, I'll be across as soon as I can get tickets. I'll ring you in the morning,

Uncle. Try not to worry. If the doctor thought there was anything to be really concerned about, he'd have told you.'

Her silent, reserved uncle seemed a little cheered by her optimism and hung up after saying, 'It will be good to have you back, Venetia.'

He wrung her heart. She hung up and turned to Ryan. In crisp, concise sentences she told him what had happened, finishing, 'I'll ring the airline and get us tickets straight away.'

'I'll do that,' he said laconically. 'You pack.'

Ten minutes later he came up the stairs to tell her that he had bookings for the next day; she was sitting on the edge of her bed wiping tears away as she methodically folded clothes.

'Ah, love, don't cry,' he said in a shaken voice, as if he couldn't bear to see her weakness.

She sniffed and said in a far from steady voice, 'I know it's stupid, but—oh, I feel a heel. She wanted me to come back, and I turned her down and now I feel as though I've put her in hospital.'

'You know perfectly well that you've done no such thing.' He sat down beside her and tilted her chin, looking deep into her eyes with compassion and an angry tenderness. 'She's going to be all right. Stop feeling guilty and tell me what I can do to help.'

She gave him a twisted smile. 'Pack your clothes,' she said. 'And eat everything in the fridge.'

CHAPTER EIGHT

THEY made the flight, after a very busy day. There was all the work attendant on closing up the house and making the other necessary arrangements to be done and John was vociferously excited, only quietening when they were actually on the big jet. By then Venetia felt as though she had been trampled by elephants.

Through it all Ryan had been collectedly efficient; in fact, she shuddered at the thought of coping without his support. As she sat watching Australia disappear beneath them she wondered wretchedly whether her aunt had shown signs of improvement. She firmed her lips, remembering the awful time just over a year ago when both Elizabeth and her grandmother had been dying. It had been a time of anguish and pain and bitter remorse...

'Stop it,' Ryan commanded softly, ignoring the stunned, appreciative gaze of the stewardess who was offering them champagne. He touched her hand in a gesture that was obscurely comforting.

Venetia had never travelled first class before, and wished tiredly that she was in a state to appreciate it. Within moments John was thirstily drinking orange juice and she was staring cautiously at the brandy Ryan had ordered.

'It makes me sleepy,' she objected, not very strongly.

'Good. You look exhausted. Did you get any sleep last night?'

'A little.'

'A very little,' he said drily, and confounded her by the tenderness of his smile. 'See if you can get some now.'

130

'John——'

'—is having the time of his life. I can look after him.'

She didn't remember drinking any of the brandy before succumbing to exhaustion and sliding into a sleep which lasted until it was time to fasten their safety-belts for the descent into Auckland.

John's face screwed up as the change in air pressure hurt his ear-drums but he didn't cry, and when they were down he heaved a long, excited sigh and said, 'When can we go in a plane again, Mummy?'

'In a few weeks,' she said, smiling at his eager, entranced expression. 'When we go back home.'

He grinned. 'Good.'

Her uncle met them, a thin, slightly stooped figure who smiled at John and asked, 'Hello. Who are you?'

John was not shy, but his voice was subdued as he answered, 'I'm John Ryan Gamble.'

Bob Gamble smiled down at him. 'I'm your Uncle Bob. If you stay long enough we might go to the zoo here. How would you like that?'

While her son was earnestly assuring him that he would like it very much Venetia firmly tamped down a multitude of uncomfortable feelings. She was not going to allow guilt to pressure her into anything silly. Like agreeing to come back to New Zealand to live.

'How's Aunt Janice?' she asked swiftly.

'Better.' Bob paused, then finished, 'In fact, she perked up as soon as she heard that you were on your way. The doctor said this afternoon that she might be allowed out in a couple of days.'

'What was the trouble?'

'Just a little turn. Her heart's not as strong as it should be, but she's not sick, and there's no need for you to worry. Your aunt is strong enough.'

He held her eyes for a second longer as though he was trying to convey a message to her. Venetia gave an infinitesimal nod. It sounded as though Janice had worked

herself up into a tizz then been frightened by her body's
reactions. She would not, Venetia thought a little sadly,
be above playing on a suspected weak heart to try to persuade Venetia to settle back in New Zealand. Such
emotional blackmail should disgust her, but she understood her aunt's emotional investment in her family and
she could not find it in her heart to be angry.

That evening Ryan looked after John while her uncle
drove Venetia to the hospital, where Janice cried over her
and told her that she felt so much better that she wanted
to go straight home so as not to miss any of the time they
were going to be there.

'Oh no, you don't,' Venetia said cheerfully. 'We can
stay for a good long holiday, so I don't want you home
until the doctor says it's OK.'

'But I am all right, it was just a silly little turn.'

Venetia hugged her aunt's thin shoulders. 'I believe
you. Nevertheless, you stay here until they give you a
clean bill of health.'

On the way home Bob asked diffidently, 'How long do
you think you'll stay, love?'

She sighed, resting her head back on to the seat. 'I
don't know. I'm not—it's an awkward situation.'

He made no attempt to persuade her as her aunt would
have done. All that he said was, 'Well, you know that we
love having you, but you must do what you want.'

'It's not exactly what I want,' she admitted. 'It's what
I think is best.'

He nodded, pulling up at a red light. The features she
shared with him were almost stern in the fading light.
'Don't let yourself be overpersuaded,' he said as he set
the car in motion again.

'No.'

Although they said no more both understood each
other. Venetia yawned, and yawned again as she walked
along the terrace towards the back door of the neat house

where her aunt and uncle had lived since they moved to Auckland.

'Bed,' came Ryan's voice from the lounger hidden under a swathe of vine at the far end of the terrace.

She jumped, but nodded. 'Yes, I'd better go. Rain, hail or aeroplane flights, John wakes at six in the morning.'

'I'll get him up,' Ryan said. 'Come and sit down, relax a little. It's a beautiful evening.'

She did as he suggested, choosing a pretty but rather uncomfortable chair beneath a festoon of chalky pink jasmine flowers. Without thinking, she said, 'Don't you have a flat in the centre of Auckland somewhere? I thought . . .' Her voice faded under his gaze.

'That I'd go to the flat?' Mockery gave a sharp edge to his smile. 'Sorry to disappoint you, but I intend to stay here at least until Janice comes home. Don't look so shattered; I have an office just off Queen Street, I'll be there for most of each day.'

She asked curiously, 'What made you decide to produce feature films? I remember once you said that you'd like to do it, but I didn't realise that you had plans made even then. It's a different thing entirely from television documentaries.'

'Not really. It's all entertainment.' He registered her sound of protest because he enlarged cynically, 'I learnt early that no one will watch a boring documentary. Making my own gave me a taste for organising, and setting up the private channel here showed me how the business and money markets in New Zealand operate. When I took the plunge the motion-picture industry in this country was just getting into its stride. It was brash and exciting and risky, as movie-making must have been in the thirties. The rest of the world is too cautious, tied to the box office.'

She nodded, understanding. He had always been attracted by challenge. From inside she could hear her uncle pottering around the kitchen, no doubt making a cup of tea. The light had faded into the cool freshness of a late spring evening, the air spiced with the scent of the jasmine which hung over the trellis. The orchids which were Bob's pride had been banished to the greenhouse at the rear of the section, but in their place were huge, brilliant amaryllis; even in the dimness beneath the pergola their enormous bold trumpets glowed in pure colours of white and scarlet and crimson, apricot and pink. Venetia gave a little sigh, unconsciously relaxing. Some things seemed never to change and the immaculate vision of her uncle's gardening was one of them.

'How does one organise a film?' she asked lazily.

Ryan chuckled. 'I started out with a computer and a room with a desk in it. After the first one brought in some money I invested in an office complete with secretary. You could say I built an infrastructure. I have a team I trust, mostly young and all eager, who do the donkey work.'

'Do you miss the immediacy of television?'

'Do you?' he countered smoothly.

She smiled. Trust Ryan to see through her question to the intent behind. 'A little. It kept the adrenalin flowing, made me feel that what I was doing was some value.'

'That's important to you, isn't it? To be valued, to have a place in the world. You don't feel that with your present work?'

'Don't put words in my mouth. I try to do as professional a job as I can within the limitations of the genre. People who read my books are as aware as anyone can be of life as it really was in the periods I choose; I may romanticise the protagonists, but the actual conditions are real.'

'You have a gritty, raw authenticity that catches the heart and satisfies the brain,' he said, surprising her. 'As for romanticising your characters, I've always considered them to be fairly lifelike. Far from cardboard. And your love scenes seem very familiar.'

She swung to look at him, uncertain whether he was sneering at her or not. He was smiling with a mocking affection, as though in a strange way he was rather touched.

'Do you think so?' she asked in a subdued voice, unsure of how to deal with him in this mood. A yawn caught her unawares and he got up and pulled her gently from her chair.

'I was teasing, but your masculine readers probably wonder if you are as superbly creative in bed as you are in print.'

Drawn into the warm strength of his body she should have resisted, but another yawn prevented any reaction and by the time she had recovered from it she was enfolded snugly in his arms, her head tucked against his shoulder.

'You're so small,' he murmured into her ear, his voice losing its harshness. 'Little and indomitable and sharp. You wear your independence like a banner. I like to look at you and know that I can kiss you free of it any time I want to. It's like owning my own small falcon, that comes only to my hand, gives up her freedom only for me.'

The words sent a shiver, half-desire, half-pain, through her. She swallowed but said with a bite, 'You like imposing your will on others.'

'Not particularly. Only on you. I think you must appeal to some atavistic, unregeneratedly primitive part of me. I need your surrender. But think, little hawk. Have I ever taken from you something you didn't want to give?'

Only my heart, she thought sadly. Only my life. And he had not taken those, she had made him a present of them, given them freely, without thought of the cost.

Her silence made him laugh soundlessly. He nuzzled the small shell of her ear and whispered, 'I like your shining honesty and your vivid love for the sensual. You appeal to the cold heart in me, lend me some of your warmth.'

Fighting against the snare of his words she said stoutly, 'Don't be silly. Your work has been characterised by a passion for truth and justice, it blazes through in everything you've done.'

'Truth and justice are cold concepts, hard and shiny with cutting edges. Is it any wonder I want you?'

She didn't know how to deal with this. He had never revealed so much before, and she was afraid that just as he despised himself for wanting her physically he would hate himself later for telling her his innermost feelings.

Slowly, her voice rueful, she said, 'I don't know that I like being used as a sort of emotional heater.'

He laughed, dropping a kiss on her hair and at that moment her uncle came to the door, peering through the dusk as he asked them if they wanted tea.

It was the perfect way to escape. 'Love some,' she told him warmly. 'And then I'm going to bed. I'm tired.'

She freed herself and walked inside, ignoring Ryan's taunting smile. Mockery she could cope with; it was his rare gentleness which unnerved her.

From the kitchen Bob said, 'Ryan, you'll be sleeping in the spare bedroom, it's the only one with two beds. Venetia, I've put you in Elizabeth's old room.'

Venetia objected. 'Shouldn't I be in the spare room if it's got two beds? John will want to sleep with me.'

Bob looked from her to Ryan, but before he could speak Ryan said lazily, 'I thought it just as well for him not to get used to sharing a room with you.' At her glittering glance he smiled and taunted, 'The evil Oedipus complex, darling. He's already jealous of me, we don't want to make it worse.'

It made sense, although his assumption that he had the right to make decisions angered her. She contented herself with another sparkling glance at him before saying with a shrug, 'I don't suppose it matters, especially as it's you he'll wake at the crack of dawn.'

Bob relaxed and, stung by his patent relief, Venetia set herself out to be pleasant. She succeeded, ignoring a sardonic smile from Ryan which made it clear that he knew what she was doing.

She slept like a log, waking to a clear, warm day which was a promise of summer. Her room—a shrine to Elizabeth complete with books and dainty china figurines—overlooked the terrace and the back yard, and she could hear through the windows John's excited voice as he chattered about the events of the day before.

Before she had a chance to do more than smile and yawn, the door swung open and Ryan appeared, almost formal in a suit which emphasised his dark attraction.

Venetia gaped, aware only too vividly of her tousled hair and unwashed face.

'Coffee,' he said laconically, and deposited the tray he carried on the pretty, delicately draped bedside table. He stood looking down at the small figure in the bed while his detached survey heated into appreciation then he bent and kissed the soft length of her throat with a reckless, heated hunger, forcing her head back into the pillow.

Venetia gasped, her hands reaching out to clutch the stuff of his sleeves. Through the material she could feel his arms, muscles rigidly flexed as though he was exerting immense will-power to keep them still.

His teeth grazed her silken skin; he muttered thickly, 'Why can't you be sweet and eager to please and amenable? Why do I have to coerce you every inch of the way? You're going to marry me eventually, Venetia. Why not just accept it?'

His arrogance converted the desire within her into splendidly liberating anger. Very crisply she retorted, 'You won't force me into a marriage I know would be a disaster. I'm not so easily intimidated. Don't confuse me with Elizabeth.'

It worked. He straightened, and stared at her defiant eyes with a savage face. 'I made that mistake once. I know better now,' he said grimly and swung around and left the room.

The coffee tasted bitter, but she drank it right down to the dregs. Then she got up and showered and dressed in a light sunfrock before following the sound of voices to where John and Bob were walking around the garden, discussing earnestly the reason for snails' shells.

They both smiled at her, but John didn't come running. Quite obviously he was perfectly at ease with her uncle.

'Where's Ryan?' she asked after exchanging greetings.

Bob looked a little cautious. 'He's gone to work. He said that he hoped to be home early so that he can take you both to see his flat.'

In a creditably calm voice she said, 'Oh, did he?'

After he, too, had left for work she and John had a pleasant day pottering around the house and the yard. In the afternoon they went to see a miraculously rejuvenated Janice, who fussed over John until he retreated behind Venetia's chair, and told them that the doctor had 'almost' promised that she could come home tomorrow.

'Good,' Venetia said in her most bracing tone. 'And no more turns. They upset Uncle Bob, he's looking tired.'

Janice looked guilty. 'I know, poor old thing. It's been a bad year. Bob can't talk about his feelings. He and you are very alike in that respect. I think if you can talk things over you get over them much faster.'

'Perhaps,' Venetia said non-committally.

Her aunt nodded. 'I'm sure of it. Still, I'm going to be perfectly all right so there's nothing for him to worry about. Have you decided yet whether to come back here to live?'

Even more non-committally Venetia said, 'No, not yet.'

'It would make things so much nicer.' Janice was wistful but almost immediately she cheered up. 'I mustn't pressure you, you're so contrary you'd cut off your nose to spite your face! How are you and Ryan getting on?'

Well, that was a question! Venetia felt her skin tighten as she said calmly, 'Not too bad.'

Her aunt nodded again. 'It *is* an awkward situation, but he had the right to know, Venetia, you can't deny that. That's why I gave him your address.'

'I had every intention of telling him.'

'When?' Janice asked, her expression shrewd as she surveyed her niece's stiff face. 'When John was old enough to start demanding answers? It would have been unfair, and you know it.'

Venetia, who did know it, said wryly, 'Yes, and you probably did the best thing. Anyway, it doesn't matter, he knows now.'

She watched her aunt's slender, hard-working fingers pleat the coverlet in a nervous mannerism. 'How do you feel about him?' the older woman asked tentatively.

'He's still an arrogant swine,' Venetia replied without heat, knowing perfectly well that if Janice had any ink-ling about the situation between Ryan and her niece she would be shocked to the core.

Sure enough, Janice sent her a swift glance before be-ginning nervously, 'He—Elizabeth——'

Venetia interrupted, determined not to venture in these dangerous waters. 'The choice was Ryan's to make, and he made it, and I haven't heard him say anything about regretting it. All I wanted was his happiness and Elizabeth gave him that.'

'So it wasn't just one of these modern affairs, all lust and then good friends when it was over. You really did love him. Oh, Venetia, it must have been . . .' She leaned towards her niece, her face soft with sympathy.

Venetia was furious with herself for that betrayal. 'It happened six years ago,' she said swiftly almost achiev-ing indifference. 'It's over.'

Quickly Janice agreed that yes, it was, and went on to tell her about the woman down the ward who shouted in her sleep every night. And so the time passed until Venetia could kiss her goodbye and leave, wondering wearily if there could ever be a time when they could open to each other without the caution that coloured all their dealings together.

It seemed unlikely. Janice would never be able to see her without remembering Elizabeth, so dearly loved, all that a daughter should be. A prickly, wilful niece was no substitute.

Ryan arrived back as John was waking from an afternoon nap, and drank coffee while Venetia stuffed their son into shorts and a T-shirt. He looked distant, preoccupied, as though it took him a little time to make the mental switch from work to leisure.

The anger of the morning was gone; in fact, he seemed to have retreated behind a wall of courtesy and reserve, emerging only to tease John amiably about the dog printed on his little shirt.

'Mummy bought it for me 'cause I want a dog,' John explained. He was beginning to accept his father although he still watched with a jealous eye whenever Ryan was near Venetia.

'If you lived with me we could get you a dog,' Ryan observed pensively. He met the kindling fury in Venetia's gaze with bland and studied incomprehension.

John looked eager and then thoughtful. He eyed his father for a long moment before saying with some of his own smoothness, 'That would be nice,' in a voice which was almost neutral.

Venetia could have cheered. She remarked coolly, 'We'll have to talk about that. John and I are very happy in Australia, aren't we, John?' John nodded, but his little face was wistful and Venetia glared at Ryan as she said, 'We had better go as it's getting late and I have to prepare dinner.'

'Oh, Bob and I have organised that, you needn't worry.'

He refused to say more and Venetia wouldn't ask again, so she was forced to go along with him with no idea of what he had planned.

In the car he said with deep amusement, 'You can stop shooting those suspicious little glances at me. I'm not likely to rape you with John here.'

'He is likely to repeat anything you say at a moment guaranteed to be inconvenient, if not embarrassing,' she retorted icily.

On cue John leaned forward from the car seat he had been strapped into and said smugly, 'A'gant swine.'

'I see what you mean.' Ryan laughed and swung the Audi Quattro into a gap which had opened in the afternoon traffic. 'Well, that's a lot more restrained than some things you've called me.'

He said nothing more to her, but occupied the time by chatting to John, giving him the names of those few vehicles he didn't already recognise. As he pulled up outside a gracious old building not very far from the centre of town he asked, 'Is this normal? Do all five-year-olds have every make of car registered on some internal computer?'

Venetia smiled. 'I think so. Jamie Dodwell certainly does. His father taught John most of his, as I'm not exactly knowledgeable.'

'Ah yes, the surrogate father.'

He said nothing more, but there was a lingering residue of unpleasantness in his voice which prevented her from pursuing the subject.

The flats had been modernised skilfully, and were luxuriously elegant; there was even a porter on duty, uncommon for New Zealand. Venetia preceded them into the lift and waited patiently while it rose the five storeys to the floor where Ryan lived in a huge, three-bedroomed flat, an opulently decorated place which bore all the marks of a professional decorator, and not, Venetia realised at the first glance, a hint of Elizabeth's personality.

Harshly, as though she had spoken the thought, Ryan said, 'I moved here three months after Elizabeth died.'

Venetia bit her lip. 'It's lovely,' she said, looking around the large sitting-room with its tasteful, neutral colour scheme.

Ryan looked cynically amused. 'It's restful. And close to work. When I move out of town I intend to sell it and get a smaller flat as a *pied-à-terre*.'

'Are you planning to do that soon?'

His dark gaze mocked her. 'Yes. I need more privacy than this place can give me. I want a farm where I can watch my children play and ride and swim.'

Stiffly she said, 'Won't you find the travelling tiresome?'

'No.'

She ran her finger along the back of the soft suede sofa, refusing to meet his eyes. John gave a hard-eyed stare around the room before asking, 'Where's my bedroom?'

'Darling——'

But Venetia's voice was overridden by Ryan's, crisp and authoritative. 'You can choose. Come and have a look.'

Each of the two spare bedrooms was empty except for a bed in each and a chest of drawers. As they entered the larger room a fire-engine shrieked its way past in the street outside and John gave an excited little gasp and ran across to the window to peer down at it. When the siren had faded into the distance he announced happily, 'This is my bedroom, Mummy. Pandy will like it best.'

Venetia cast a fulminating look at Ryan, but her voice was steady as she said, 'That's nice. If you come to stay with Daddy you and Pandy can sleep here.'

'Good.' John was pleased but said cunningly, 'Where will you sleep?'

Again, before Venetia could say anything Ryan interposed in a provocative tone, 'Come and see.'

Ryan's bedroom was the only room in the house with any mark of his personality. It was big, with windows which overlooked a leafy avenue and a park, and the bed was wide and richly covered in a silk spread in darkest chocolate. The rest of the room formed a cool, restrained setting for the lovely bed; above it, surprising Venetia, was an Indian wall hanging in the glowing brilliant colours of the east, sensuous, erotic, with harem women and dancers entertaining a solemn potentate.

'The bathroom's through there,' Ryan said, waving a lean hand towards a door in the wall. 'As you can see, there's plenty of wardrobe space. I thought we could turn the third bedroom into an office for you.'

She looked straight at him and said evenly, 'That's enough.'

He nodded and she thought she saw lurking in his eyes a kind of amused sympathy as though he understood her frustration at his unfair tactics. Perhaps he did, but she knew him well enough to appreciate that, sympathy or not, he would continue trying to back her into a corner so that she was trapped with no way out but marriage. And he was ruthless, so using his son as lever would not upset him.

'Which reminds me,' he said smoothly, 'I want you to come to a party with me tomorrow night. One of the financial corporations I have dealt with—and may want to use again—are entertaining a scion of Arabian royalty. You can buy something to wear tomorrow morning, then I'll take you both to the beach.'

'No.'

He smiled, all ironbound determination. 'Yes, darling,' he said. 'Don't put me to the bother of making you do it.'

Her eyes were cold and empty. 'I won't,' she said. 'Find someone else to entertain your financiers.'

He smiled again, without humour. 'I want you.'

It was a threat, all the more effective for being delivered in a low, almost flat voice. Venetia shivered and turned away, heading for the door of the bedroom. John had preceded her and could be heard making siren sounds in the room he had chosen for his own.

'Venetia . . .'

His hand on her arm was the final straw. She turned on him, her eyes spitting sparks, jerking herself free from his grasp. 'Leave me alone,' she gritted, 'just leave me alone!'

His hand tightened then fell away. He was astute enough to know when he had pushed her far enough, although a narrowed glance up into his dark, harshly constricted features was enough to tell her how much he wanted to force her to surrender. You marry him, she told herself fiercely, and you won't be able to call your soul your own!

But somehow, in spite of all her determination, she found herself the next morning being ushered into the fitting-room of an exclusive boutique off Queen Street by a stunningly elegant middle-aged woman. Only half an hour later she was back in the Audi with the most expensive dress she had ever bought reposing in its striped box in the boot.

'Forgiven me?' Ryan asked, slanting her a heavy-lidded look.

She said with empty courtesy, 'Oh yes, although I'll never wear the thing again. I paid for it myself.'

He nodded. 'I thought you probably would. The idea of taking anything from me fills you with horror, doesn't it?'

Put like that it sounded almost petty. 'No, but if you want a gracious acceptance you shouldn't run roughshod over me.'

The deep voice warmed, became coloured with irony. 'That's the only way to deal with you,' he said easily. 'I want you to look good because most of Auckland's upper crust, as well as few scrabbling desperately to get there, will be at this thing tonight. I won't have them looking down on you.'

She frowned, but pleasure at his protectiveness robbed her irritation of its sting. 'Nobody,' she informed him, calmly, 'looks down on me, because I won't allow them to.'

He lifted an eyebrow at her before pitching his voice to reach the back seat. 'Travelling well there, John?'

'I can see a beach,' John reminded him politely.

'Wait a little while longer and you'll be able to see the one we're going to.'

He took them to Takapuna Beach on the North Shore, a long sweep of sand overlooking Rangitoto Channel and the island of the same name. It was almost deserted except for several people down at the other end, so John was able to run yelling across the sand after seagulls while Venetia anointed her skin liberally with sunblock and spread herself out on the rug Ryan had removed from the back of the car.

He stripped off his shirt and sat down beside her, his eyes hooded as he watched the little boy in all his joyous effervescence. The sea breeze lifted a tendril of dark hair across his brow. Venetia looked away, disturbed by the almost irresistible desire to smooth it back. He was too close, all sleek and gleaming in the sun, broad shoulders rippling with muscles, the strong arms loosely wrapped around his knees as he watched his son from beneath lowered eyelids. Her mouth dried. She stared stonily out to sea, hating the sweet agony of need which fountained through her.

As she dressed for the party that night Venetia thought that seldom had she passed such a pleasant day. John had run and built castles, made friends with three dogs and their owners, warmed to his father, paddled and splashed, his shrieks of laughter ringing through the salty air. Now, exhausted, he lay sound asleep.

And when they came home, there waiting for them had been Janice, rosy-faced and mischievous. Bob had called in to the hospital on his way home from work and picked her up. 'No,' she said in answer to Ryan's amused enquiry, 'I did not discharge myself. They were glad to see me go!'

She and Ryan had a pleasant, teasing relationship; that he was fond of her was obvious, and just as obvious was her admiration for him. He seemed to relax in her company—as, Venetia thought, he must have with Elizabeth.

The dress she had chosen that morning was a fluid slither of silk which made the most of her blonde hair and slender figure, falling in graceful folds to just below the knees. The colour, pure solid scarlet, was as eye-catching as the style was simple. With it she carried a bag made of the same material and wore little scarlet sandals.

'You look stunning,' her aunt enthused from her bed when Venetia posed in the doorway for her.

Venetia said wryly, 'I'm so short I have to wear simple styles, but I like a colour that shouts for attention.'

'It shouldn't suit you, but it does. Off you go, and have a lovely time. Make sure you get a good look at the Sheikh so you can tell me about him.' When Venetia hesitated in the doorway her aunt said briskly, 'No, I do not need you here. Bob is quite capable of keeping an eye on me, and you know John won't wake up.'

Venetia laughed because unerringly Janice had hit on the two things that were worrying her. 'I'll see you in the morning. Goodnight.'

Excitement bubbled lightly through her in a delicious euphoria. Beneath her lashes her eyes gleamed like jewels, vivid and shockingly bright. She looked like a siren, beckoning, a little dangerous.

Ryan rose to his feet as she came into the room, tall and attractively rakish in evening clothes, but the look he gave her was arrested, as if he had forgotten how lovely she could be. She smiled at him with slow, mischievous allure and watched his eyes darken to onyx as they swept her face.

'Let's go,' he said and held out a hand.

First she kissed Bob goodbye, then allowed Ryan to lead her out into the deepening dusk to the car. The party was being held in the city's newest and most upmarket hotel, built since Venetia's day, and she was looking forward to seeing it. As Ryan steered the car beneath the portico a group of people stepped from the Rolls-Royce ahead, elegantly dressed, very aware of themselves and their surroundings. A little smile curved Venetia's mouth and was reflected by Ryan.

'Do we look as self-conscious and haughty?' she asked, then answered herself, 'No, you'd look at home anywhere.'

'Perhaps journalism provides a rapid course in sophistication, because so would you.'

It was a compliment she fully intended to savour, but later, when she had time. As the commissionnaire opened the door she gave him an urchin's grin and stepped out on to the footpath.

CHAPTER NINE

IT was the kind of party which was more fun to recall than to experience. No expense had been spared, the guests were fashionable and very much on their best behaviour, the Arabian Prince intriguing although not particularly talkative, and the surroundings as opulent as unlimited money could make them.

Everyone appeared to be having a wonderful time, and they watched each other all the time to make sure that no one was getting more of the limelight than they deserved. Those people who recognised Venetia regarded her with avid interest, shooting fascinated, hopeful glances at her from beneath lowered lashes, turning away as they whispered.

Venetia ignored them, but the sick feeling in her stomach would not go away. This was only a slight taste of the sort of unwelcome interest which would be engendered if she was stupid enough to come back to New Zealand. Her heart quailed at the thought of what would happen if these interested bystanders ever laid eyes on John.

It was, she thought drearily, an aspect of the situation which no one else seemed to have considered. Ryan might have, he knew the sort of world he inhabited, but he would be confident of his ability to protect both her and their son. Certainly he had no intention of allowing any wolves at her back this night; he stayed with her, uncaring of how possessive his behaviour must seem.

The party stopped being a strain and turned into a nightmare half way through the evening as she was coming back from the cloakroom.

148

One word did it. Her name.

'Venetia?'

The masculine voice was tentative, half astonished, but the shock of recognition drove all colour from her skin.

'Sean,' she whispered.

He recovered faster than she. He was already smiling, the same teasing, vitally attractive smile which had caused such havoc in her silly eighteen-year-old heart.

'I thought I regonised that hair,' he said softly, his startling blue eyes searching her face. 'Come and dance with me.'

For a moment she hesitated, then said, 'Why not?' and went into his arms.

Half-way around the floor she asked warily, 'What are you doing here?'

'Oh, I've just returned from exile in America. Brett—do you remember him, my stuffy cousin? Ah yes, I see you do. He's suggested I take up the reins on one of the family properties, a cattle and sheep station up north. As I've been a good boy he let me come with him tonight.' He chuckled wickedly. 'He's going to rue it when he sees us together. You're looking good, Venetia. How's things?'

'Fine,' she said airily, closing her eyes briefly at the lie.

The Sean she had known before, the boy she had married, would have accepted that at face value. He had been selfish and self-absorbed as only the young can be. This older Sean looked at her for a long moment, the vivid blue eyes unexpectedly sympathetic, before he gave a crooked smile and said, 'If you say so.'

She returned the smile unwillingly, hurrying into speech. 'Tell me what you've been doing since——'

He supplied the words she found hard to say. 'Since our divorce? Well, I went to Massey College and took a degree, and then was sent off to a ranch in Texas for some overseas experience. Originally I was meant to stay there only a year, but I was having too good a time to come home.'

'A cowboy?'

'You better believe it, ma'am,' he drawled in a passable Texan accent.

Venetia laughed, and laughed even more at some of the tall tales he regaled her with; beneath the laughter she was astonished that she should be so relaxed with him. He had been a sullen, antagonistic husband, but then who would not have been, forced by his own sense of honour and her aunt and uncle into marriage at the age of nineteen! She discovered that after all these years she was able to like him again. It was with this knowledge and the relief it brought showing in her unguarded face that she looked past him and met Ryan's level gaze.

There was not a flicker of emotion in the dark eyes, yet she flinched as though she had been hit.

'And who,' Sean asked without missing a beat, 'is that? Your husband?'

'No.' What impelled her she didn't know, but the words tumbled out before she could stop them. 'The father of my son. Elizabeth's husband.'

'Christ,' he said on a long breath.

She dragged her eyes free from Ryan's and said wearily, 'I seem to repeat myself. You'd have thought I'd learn.'

Sean hugged her close. 'Want to talk about it?'

'No, not really.'

But he asked, 'What does Elizabeth feel about it?'

'She's dead.' She couldn't leave it at that, so she told him briefly what had happened. When her voice finally ran down he said nothing and she looked up to see compassion in his expression.

'Don't pity me,' she said curtly.

It vanished. 'Oh, I don't dare, you never could cope with pity. I remember how after you lost the baby you retreated into your own private hell and I didn't know what to do.' After a moment's hesitation he finished, 'I hate thinking of the way I behaved. It's too late to say I'm sorry, but I am.'

She felt a surge of affection for him. 'We were both so hopelessly young.'

He frowned then asked, 'But what's going on now? That's no brotherly glare we're getting from Tall-dark-and-handsome looming over there on the sidelines. If looks could kill, I'd be gasping my last on the floor.'

Only Sean would have the audacity to dismiss Ryan's deadly stare so lightly. In spite of her unease Venetia gave a choke of laughter, but when she spoke determination ran like steel through her words. 'Nothing is happening. I married once because of a child; I can find enough fresh mistakes to make without having to repeat any!'

As the music stopped he asked urgently, 'Are you in love with him?'

She said nothing, but after one look at her shuttered face he said, 'I see. Close-mouthed as ever, aren't you? That's one tough-looking *hombre* over there, love. If you ever need any help, give me a call.' She was touched and it showed in the glowing glance she lifted to him. Wryly he finished, 'But you'll cope alone. No wonder your aunt and uncle were at their wits' end with you. You're like a little fighting cock; a far cry from Elizabeth. She always reminded me of a mother hen, all placidly domestic.'

She smiled, mulling over his comparison as the music stopped and they walked across the floor. She made no cowardly attempt to avoid Ryan, although his anger burned into her like the brilliant flames in the heart of sea ice.

The two men spoke together with a kind of wintry politeness until Sean said cheerfully, 'Must go, or my big cousin Brett will come gunning for me.' His bright, knowing gaze moved from Venetia to the man beside her; his eyes danced with mischief as he finished, 'You know

where to find me if you need me, Venetia. Nice to have
met you, Fraine.'

As a parting shot it couldn't have been bettered.
Venetia felt the sudden stiffening of Ryan's frame and in
spite of herself sent a furious glance at Sean. His grin
widened. Not at all abashed, he nodded at Ryan and took
himself off, the light glinting on his arrogantly held blond
head.

'I don't need to ask who that was.' The tone was completely neutral, but it failed to hide the corrosive contempt behind the words.

Suddenly exhausted, she retorted brusquely, 'No.'

He made no reply. After a moment Venetia looked up;
a white line around his mouth stood out. For a painful
second his fingers bit into her arm. He was not looking
at her; his eyes followed Sean's straight back across the
room and his mouth compressed into total ruthlessness.
Then he released her, saying distantly, 'Let's get out of
here.'

She accepted his curtailment of the evening without
protest, but when she realised that he was taking her to
his flat she opened her mouth to object. However, one
glance at his iron-hard profile kept her silent until their
arrival.

Once inside the sitting-room Venetia sat down gratefully on the sofa, watching him with a careful face as he
poured drinks, brandy for her, his usual whisky.

Her hands curved around the glass but she made no
attempt to drink, unlike Ryan who drained almost half
of his before he at last looked across at her.

'Tell me,' he commanded with deliberate and icy restraint, 'what you think of your ex-husband after all these
years.'

The brandy swirled, amber and glowing, in the heavy
crystal of the glass. Staring into the warm depths she replied tonelessly, 'He's grown up. It was barely a marriage. I was eighteen, he was one year older.'

'What the hell were Bob and Janice doing to agree to that?'

'Oh, they insisted on it. We may have been little more than children, but we were old enough to make a baby. Sean was chivalrous enough to go along with their arrangements.'

'And you?'

She shrugged, lowering her gaze again to the brandy. 'I was young, I was frightened. Protesting didn't get me anywhere, and I thought——' her voice wavered but strengthened immediately '—I thought it would be best for the baby.'

'And you miscarried.'

She bit her lip and had to steady her voice again. 'After that there was no longer any need for the marriage. We were divorced by the time I was twenty.'

Harshly he demanded, 'Were you in love with him?'

'No,' she whispered.

He strode across the room and caught her chin in hard, hurting fingers, dragging it up so that he could see into her face. The unshed tears glittering beneath her lashes rendered him blurry and distorted but she saw the change in his expression. He muttered an expletive under his breath and the fingers beneath her chin gentled as he came down beside her on the sofa.

She gulped and he pulled her across his lap, holding her there as she struggled, until at last the rigidity left her small, stiff body and she began to weep, difficult tearing sobs, painful to hear.

He held her gently, almost tenderly, until the sobs eased, and then he gave her his handkerchief and waited while she mopped up. When she was once more in control of her emotions he asked, 'Why do you feel guilty, Venetia?'

She shuddered. 'When it was over, all I could feel was relief. Janice said—it was all for the best, and I knew Sean was relieved. So was I. I knew I was too young to be responsible for a baby. But—I felt as though I'd killed her...'

He reached a long arm around her to pick up the glass of brandy he had put on the side table. 'Drink it,' he insisted when she shook her head, and held it to her lips until half of it was gone.

The spirit hit her stomach and spread, warm and comforting, through her veins. She muttered, 'I'm sorry.'

'For crying? Is this the first time you've allowed yourself to mourn for her?'

'I don't cry easily.'

'You don't do anything easily.' He took the glass from her fingers and put it down. Venetia moved away from the too-beguiling strength of his shoulder and sat with her head downcast, afraid to let him see her face. She could feel him watching her. 'Is tonight the first time you've seen him since you left him?'

She nodded, uneasy but valiant.

His voice sharpened. 'And what did you feel when you saw him?'

'Surprise.'

'Don't play games,' he warned her silkily.

A flare of resentment brought her head up. He had no right to poke around among her emotions! A second later, after she had taken the measure of the hard compulsion in his features, she surrendered. 'Liking,' she said in a small voice.

'That's all?'

His sceptical question made her shift cautiously, as tense as an animal slowly being forced into a cage. 'That's all I ever felt for him. That, and a sudden surge of hormones to the head one day.'

It had only taken that once for her to conceive John, too. It seemed, she thought savagely, that she had Elizabeth's share of the family fertility as well as her own.

'But all you felt tonight was liking?'

She reacted to the merciless probing with defiance. Her heavy head stiffened on her slender neck; she stared angrily into his darkly demanding face, her mouth tightening. 'That's all,' she said flatly, daring him to continue.

That white line was about his mouth again, but this time it did not seem to denote anger. He got to his feet as if he could not bear to stay close to her and paced across the room, asking with frozen distinctness, 'How many men had you slept with before you met me, Venetia?'

Her shoulders lifted in a weary little shrug. 'One,' she said clearly.

To her incredulous amazement she saw him flinch. Without turning he reached for his glass and drained the whisky as if he was dying of thirst. Then he said in a remote voice, 'Why did you lie to me? Why did you let me believe that I was one of a procession of men who'd lost themselves in that passionate little body?'

She too drank, and waited a little while the brandy loosened her tongue, paving the way for the truth. 'I fell in love with you. I wanted to be the sort of woman you found attractive, and from what I knew of your previous liaisons that seemed to mean experience. But I didn't lie to you. You never asked me.'

'So you were almost totally inexperienced?'

She nodded. 'Yes. I knew you wouldn't want a woman who was the next best thing to a virgin.' She laughed softly, ironically. 'And then you fell in love with Elizabeth, who was the real thing. Amusing, isn't it?'

He swung around, his face drawn and rigid with suppressed emotion. 'Do you realise what you did?'

'I've had six years to realise,' she told him calmly. 'But even if I had told you of my lack of experience, would it have made any difference?'

He turned away again and said angrily, 'Of course it damned well would! You went to a considerable amount of trouble to present yourself as a tough little sophisticate. I wasn't into self-denial, especially as——' he stopped, then finished in a goaded voice '—especially as you were a challenge I couldn't resist. Have there been any men since John was born?'

Tendrils of fear wove their way through her. She said quickly, 'It's no use rehashing the past. It's over, done with, dead. But I won't marry you for John's sake. At long last I'm beginning to learn from experience.'

Ryan set his glass down with a sudden, sharp movement; the clink as it hit the table indicated his unusual tension. He stood for a second looking at it, his profile aureoled by the lamp; it was a cameo of force and resolution, fierce as a hawk's, with all the clear-cut power of his masculine authority. Slowly, carefully, Venetia huddled back into the sofa. She could smell danger, taste it coppery over her tongue.

Then he turned his head and looked at her, and she cried out and jumped to her feet, impelled to flight by the searing purpose she read in his face.

Ryan caught her before she had gone three steps. His hands slid from that first jolting impact on her shoulders beneath her arms to cover her breasts. He said, 'No, the past is *not* dead. It's haunted me ever since you left,' and pulled her back against the hard, aroused length of his body.

She twisted and fought, tearing at those merciless hands with her nails, desperately trying to summon up details of a self-defence course she had taken long ago, but although he didn't hurt her he refused to let her go and at last she stopped and stood still, gasping.

'Why must you do everything the hard way?' he demanded, almost tiredly. 'I don't want you to hurt yourself.'

'But you don't mind hurting me,' she returned fiercely in a voice ragged and edged with pain. 'Don't do this, Ryan. It's not going to solve anything.'

'Probably not,' he agreed, 'but I'm afraid it's too late to stop now.'

His mouth came down on to the skin at the side of her throat. He said obscurely, 'I have to,' and bit gently, sensuously into the tender junction between neck and shoulder.

Venetia shuddered. The satin texture of her skin pulled into goose-flesh and pure sensation tore through her like a ripping bolt of silk. With a reckless defiance of the consequences she choked, 'I won't be used as a substitute for Liz. I *won't*!'

'Elizabeth has been dead for over a year,' he said against her skin. 'This is just between you and me, Venetia. It always has been. No one else has ever had any place in this.'

Wondering what he meant, she began to shake her head, but he turned her and she saw on his face the hard mask of passion, impersonal, implacable. A flare of response lit up her expression; in the reckless glitter of his half-closed eyes she saw his knowledge that the dark sweep of colour along his high cheekbones was replicated in hers, the probing incitement of his curled mouth mirrored in her softer, more vulnerable curve.

Her brain clouded; her taut skin was heated by the roseate hues of passion; she put up a shaking finger to touch his predatory mouth and then sighed and relaxed into him with the strangest sensation of homecoming.

The first kiss was gentle, seducingly sweet, the latent brutality she remembered nowhere in evidence. As if she were seventeen again he teased her mouth open, tasting the softness, all of his concentration focused through his mouth, his tongue.

Venetia's eyes closed in dazed pleasure; she gave in to the dark tide of splendour which rolled over her, at once relaxing and stimulating, tightening her nerves in delicious tension, yet easing out all apprehension until she could think of nothing else but this man and his hands, his mouth, the incredible attraction in his taut restraint.

He wooed her with tenderness and control, kissing her mouth and the lovely, stubborn line of her jaw and chin, relearned the shape of her ears and stabbed with a wicked tongue into the centre of the delicate whorls, sending a violent tremor coursing through her, summoning a shuddering wildness which knew no shame, no inhibitions. Teasing, wilfully provocative, she pulled open his shirt and wound her arms around him, thrusting her small slenderness against him in a quick, sinuous movement of her hips before pulling away to watch him with a smile which made a thousand promises.

'I want you,' he muttered starkly, his narrowed eyes glittering. 'All of you, everything, all of your passion and laughter and anger, all for me, only mine...'

Did he know what he was saying? It didn't seem possible, for he was a sophisticated man, such primitive, heady words sounded strange on his tongue.

By now Venetia didn't care. Her hands were searching, appreciating the feel of sleek skin over muscle, the fine roughness of his chest, the warmth and potent virility of his frame against hers.

He smelt so good, she thought fuzzily, leaning forward to touch her seeking mouth to his chest. Warm, roused male, the most powerful aphrodisiac in the world... With her tongue she traced a little path through the thatch of hair, finding the tight male nipple. He said something deep in his throat, then groaned, and his arm hardened about her.

The world spun; she looped her arms around his neck and watched his face as he carried her out of the room into the dark bedroom. A light flowered against her quickly closed eyelids and she made a little noise of protest as he set her on her feet.

'Can't you stand up?' he asked, half laughing, wholly absorbed as he slid her dress from her shoulders.

'Of course I can.'

Was that her voice? Heavy and husky and slow, as mesmerised by the sensations rioting through her as he was; she watched while with trembling hands he stripped her, each touch of his fingers followed by his mouth until he was kneeling before her naked figure, his worshipping lips against her breast.

'You are so beautiful,' he murmured. 'I hadn't forgotten ... Venetia ...'

Almost delirious with pleasure her knees buckled at the unashamed yearning in his words. He caught her and put her on the bed before tearing himself free from his clothes, the gentle lamplight falling on his body in a wash of copper and bronze, sliding lovingly over the play of skin above taut muscle, over lean strength and a beauty of form which had been imprinted on her senses, in her very cells since the first time she had seen him.

Venetia drew a deep, painful breath. Her tongue touched lips suddenly dry, and she felt the sweet ache in her bones transmute into a hunger so intense that she cried out softly with the agony of it. She held out her arms in a gesture as old as womankind, and he came down into them with a desperate, urgent need.

She was ready, she needed nothing more, but slowly, tenderly, with an erotic finesse which soon had her moaning in ecstasy and frustration, he made love to her as if she were the virgin of seventeen she had recalled for him.

And although her body cried out for fulfilment she did not try to hurry him. Somehow she knew what he was doing. His hands moved quietly, gently, framed her face as he kissed her, slid to cup the high mounds of her breasts.

He kissed the place where her heart threatened to burst through the confines of her body, the soft hollows in her throat, the gentle width of her shoulders, sensitising skin already heated and tender. Tentatively she touched him, running her hand to his hip, but he shook his head and when she ignored him and explored further he caught her wrists and held her hands above her head so that she was laid out before him: a small slender figure of rose and ivory, vulnerable on the rich, dark sheets of the big bed.

'Ryan,' she whispered as his head moved down to her breasts; for a moment it rested there as sweetly as a child's, until he turned the rough silk of his face against her skin and the heat of his mouth enclosed the peaked nipple and she groaned, a spasm of pleasure rippling through her.

He had never been a gentle lover. Her responses, powerful and uninhibited, had elicited a like reaction from him. She had given no quarter and quite often both had been bruised by the end of their lovemaking.

So this tenderness, this gentleness, was unexpected. He wooed instead of demanding and used all of his expertise to coax from her a response she had never before experienced. Even as her body strained in an urgent bow against him he remained tormentingly in command, caressing her as though she was innocent, easily startled by passion.

Only when the fine torture urged her to wrench her wrists free did he use his strength against her, holding her a prisoner still.

'Ryan,' she begged in a husky, wild voice, 'I can't bear this. Please let me . . . I want to . . .'

He didn't seem to hear her. His mouth found the indentation of her narrow waist, the small, tight hollow of her navel, the gentle flare of her hips. Every muscle in her body tightened in a spasm of need as his hand found the secret recesses of her body and entered, knowledgeable, cunning, the power of ecstasy in his touch, in his mouth, in the weight of his body.

His name burst from her lips on a long, moaning note and she began to fling her head from side to side on the pillow, lost in the dark reaches of passion.

As if the sound were the signal he needed to hear, the restraint he had imposed on himself cracked, shattered into nothingness. He took her on a surge of dynamic power, stamped her with the strength of his desire, called forth a response so direct and vital that she convulsed almost immediately, sobbing, her small, twisting body racked with glory. At the same moment he went with her into that spinning, rapturous world of the senses, and aeons later came with her down from it, his breath as painful in his chest as hers, his heart joining hers in a tumult of satiety.

She had no idea how long they lay like that. The sweat they mingled dried, he felt her shiver and pulled up the blankets without moving more than a long arm. His weight pushed her into the mattress, but when he made to move she made an inarticulate little noise and tightened her arms about him.

Dreamily she thought she could feel the slow tides of life as they pumped through his body; dreamily she pondered on the fact that only he could force such an overpowering sensuality from her.

At last their breathing slowed, the heavy, driving beat of each heart easing into normality, and this time when he moved she let him go, yawning delicately as he tucked her into him so that she lay in the strong cage of his arms, his chin resting on the top of her head.

'Now, sleep,' he said in a voice which sounded as though he was drugged with satisfaction and exhaustion.

When she woke it was to the infuriating brr-brr of a telephone. She turned anxiously, completely at a loss, and froze as her body collided with another. Heat washed over her. Her eyes flew open in time to see Ryan stretch out a lazy arm and pick up the receiver and bring it to his ear.

'Yes? Oh, Janice . . . Yes, she's here.' His lashes lifted; impassively he surveyed Venetia's appalled face. 'Do you want to speak to her? Oh, I see. Yes, tell him we'll be home in half an hour.'

In bitter silence Venetia waited until he had replaced the receiver before saying icily, 'Why?'

He was watching her with a narrow, flinty smile. At her question he hesitated, choosing his words. 'That's what we've both been waiting for,' he said at last, his look very keen and hard as it probed her expression.

She just stared at him. He turned over on to his back and linked his hands behind his head to gaze assessingly up at the ceiling. 'I want my son,' he said calmly.

'Sleeping with me is not going to get you your son. For heaven's sake, I'm not weak enough to be coaxed into marrying you just because you're a magnificent lover!'

His mouth curved in an unkind smile. 'When you lie beneath me in my bed you'll say anything I want you to, and you know it.'

Venetia jerked upright, rigid with fury, her eyes burning him with golden fire. 'You are despicable!' she stormed, uncaring that she was naked. 'My God, I wish I could do to you what you're doing to me!'

He laughed, actually laughed, and with genuine amusement, saying as she stared at him in outrage and shock, 'Darling, I didn't realise that you think I'm a better actor than Olivier; I can assure you I'm not. You must know what you make me feel. I'm every bit as vulnerable as you are. I thought I'd shown you that last night. However, if you want to be reassured . . .'

He reached towards her with amusement and passion in the black depths of his eyes. Venetia hesitated, then jumped from the bed as if he was the devil himself, and fled into the bathroom with the sound of his low, confident laughter following her.

It was embarrassing to have to meet her aunt's reproachful eyes, but within minutes Ryan had charmed Janice from shocked distaste to a resigned acquiescence.

He did not have quite such luck with John, who carefully ignored them both for almost half an hour until he approached Venetia and with a lowering face demanded that Ryan go back home. 'Now,' he said bluntly, just in case anyone failed to understand him.

'I,' Ryan told Venetia calmly, 'am going to the zoo.'

This was a master stroke. Watching the chagrin in her son's expression being succeeded rapidly by thoughtfulness, Venetia could only applaud Ryan's tactics.

'Perhaps Mummy and me could go to the zoo too,' John suggested cunningly.

Venetia shook her head. 'No, I have to write letters.'

His face fell. After a moment or two of profound thought he peeped through his lashes at his father. 'Is there elephants there?'

'Two. A little one and a big one.' Ryan sounded quite indifferent.

'How long are you going to be there?'

'Long enough to see the elephants. And the giraffes.'

Without a struggle John cast resentment to the winds. 'I would like to see them,' he said grandly, approaching his father.

'Get your shoes and we'll be off.'

When they had gone Venetia faced her uncle and aunt with the aloof, cold cast to her features which had always been her shield against their disappointment.

But Janice was defensive, saying on a rush of words, 'When John came running in to tell us that you weren't in your bed we were worried.'

'Yes, I'm sorry, I should have rung.'

'What you do is your own concern,' Bob said with an admonitory glance at his wife, 'but John didn't like it.'

Venetia sighed. 'I hope he gets over this jealousy.'

'I don't think he's so much jealous as possessive,' her uncle said drily, adding, 'Like his father.'

She nodded, and went along to her room, wondering bleakly how much longer she was going to feel guilty be-

cause she didn't live up to their expectations. Fortunately her excuse for staying behind had been true; within
a few minutes she had pushed everything to the back of
her mind and was lost in the letter she had promised Kay
Dodwell, only to be interrupted well before it was finished by a tap at the door.

'Yes?' she asked, more abruptly than necessary.

Janice came in and shut the door behind her. 'I wondered if you had any washing to do.'

'No,' Venetia said slowly. 'I put it all in the basket.'

Janice came across the room and looked interestedly
at the portable typewriter, ran her fingers over the desk,
presumably to check it for dust, and tidied up one or two
papers.

'What is it?' Venetia asked after a moment, re-
straining the impatience which ate into her.

'I—are you planning to marry Ryan?'

'No.' Her voice was without intonation, she sat very
still, waiting for her aunt to finish and go away so that
she could lose herself in the sanctuary which the letter
offered her. While she was writing she had to concentrate.

Janice had lovely hands, long and slender with tapered
fingers. They moved over the desk and then back to her
sides, where they folded in on themselves. In a difficult
voice Janice asked, 'Did you—last night——?'

'We made love.'

A little breath hissed between her aunt's lips. The
clenched hands tightened still more. 'I see. But you don't
want to marry him?'

'I'm not into masochism,' Venetia said tiredly, hating
Ryan for putting her in this position, hating herself for
being so much a captive of her desires that she was unable to refuse what he offered her.

Janice sat down on the bed, her green eyes anxious and
pained. 'Doesn't he love you?'

'No, he doesn't. He wants me, he finds me very good for a convenient roll in the hay, we mesh very nicely that way, but if we married I would always know that that was all he felt for me, and it is not enough. I'm greedy, I want it all. I always have. And because I rather think it would kill me to marry a man who looks at me and sees Liz, I'm not going to marry him. It's as easy as that.'

As if she had not heard Janice said quietly, 'He used to treat Elizabeth as though she was a charming, affectionate child to whom he was devoted. He doesn't look at you like that.' She flushed and looked embarrassed. 'I'm not a particularly passionate person, although your uncle and I have a very happy marriage, but I know passion when I see it. Venetia, Ryan drowns in you, his eyes eat you, he watches you all the time. Sometimes he looks desperate.'

'It's known as sex, it doesn't last.'

'If it's lasted for six years...' Her voice trailed away as she saw her niece's obdurate expression. But instead of leaving it at that she took a deep sustaining breath and plunged on. 'I never thought you were a coward, Venetia. Or are you punishing him for marrying Elizabeth instead of you?'

Venetia's hand clenched suddenly on the desk. She could not hide the flash of gold fire beneath her lashes, but her voice was icily composed as she replied, 'I won't be manipulated into doing something I feel is wrong for me.'

'You mean you won't admit that it is black, stubborn pride that is stopping you from trying to heal things.' Janice got to her feet and walked back to the door, pausing just inside it to deliver her parting shot. 'I know it's going to be difficult, but you might just as well learn to compromise, Venetia. Ryan is going to be part of your life; he won't let John go now he's found him. I don't know how he feels about you, but it seems to me that you can give him something Elizabeth didn't even know he needed. You love him. You always have. Is your love such a mean thing that you would deprive John of the father he's going to need very much from now on just to satisfy your pride?'

CHAPTER TEN

THE letter to Kay finished, Venetia leaned back in the chair with her eyes closed. She was exhausted and depressed, yet her mind wandered back to the night before, to Ryan's amazing tenderness and her turbulent, shatteringly sweet response.

Could she reject that supreme pleasure, cut it from her life because she wanted more than just the sensual magic?

She got to her feet, wanting nothing more than to walk away her fretting, tormented thoughts. Through the open window she could see across the garden, the neatly clipped hedge, and on past the red roof of the house next door. It was sunny and hot and, judging by the shrieks of laughter she could hear through the trees, the neighbours had decided to christen their swimming pool for the season.

Her aunt's words rang in her head. Was she suffering from wounded pride, a desire for revenge? Sighing, she rested her forehead on the cool glass. Did it matter that Ryan had loved Elizabeth?

For years she had forbidden her mind to stray into those paths; it hurt, now, to examine her actions with the clear, incisive logic which had made her a good reporter. And what she saw there hurt even more. Yes, it was pride and probably a nasty case of family rivalry which had made her so uncompromising. And yes, she did want to punish him, because he had been happy and she had lived with loneliness.

Did it matter that he would never love her as he had loved Liz? Oh yes, she thought, drenched in anguish, it mattered. But he wanted her and she, who had somewhat vaingloriously prided herself on her strength, she could cope with being second-best.

Which left her to cope with the deep-seated resentment because she could make him gasp out his desire in an agony of sensation. He had such a fundamental need to be in command, as inherent in him as his arrogant possessiveness, and the incandescent force of the reaction she roused in him was a direct threat to that need.

It would not be easy to convince him that he was not diminished in any way by his uncontrollable hunger for her, but surely when he learned that she would never use his need as a weapon he would begin to accept it and eventually perhaps the resentment would diminish and fade away. And that really left her with only one question.

Was her love strong enough to cope? A brilliant smile lit her small face. Oh yes, she was strong enough to cope with anything! Especially one arrogant, moody man who did not yet realise just how binding the ties of a family could be. And she would make for him the sort of loving home which would compensate for the deep-rooted insecurity of his childhood. She could do that. John would help and so would the other children she would give him.

So she would accept his proposal. And even as she made the decision she knew she was only acknowledging the inevitable.

They came back cheerful and slightly sunburned from their trip to the zoo. John was extremely talkative about the delights he had seen, among which the elephants and an ice-cream figured largely. And from the way he looked at Ryan it was clear that the breakthrough had been made.

While Janice bore John off to the bathroom to wash his sticky face Ryan looked at Venetia's small, straight figure, almost childlike in a brief sunfrock, and asked coolly, 'Have you made up your mind?'

'I suppose I'll have to marry you.' As soon as the words were out she realised how they must sound, but it was too late to call them back.

'Don't do me any favours!'

The lash of bitterness in his tone caught her up short. Had Elizabeth done him favours, or was that hostility based on his childhood perceptions of neglect? She would never know, and if she did not banish the thought of Elizabeth to the past where it belonged, a marriage between them had no chance.

Soberly, trying to lighten the moment, she said, 'Tell me that in a year's time! I'm far from domesticated, and you will have realised by now that John is no sweet, cuddly little boy!'

His mouth twisted into a mockery of a smile. 'Sorry, I've been less than flattering to your dutiful surrender, haven't I? Put it down to surprise; I had expected it to take much more bullying before you gave in. Shall we seal our arrangement the usual way?'

Made uneasy by the bite in his voice she stepped back, but he was having none of that. Anger gleamed cold as the light of a dead star in the darkness of his eyes, but there was passion too and it was the passion she responded to, accepting the hard force of his kiss with a reluctant ardour which turned the subtle cruelty into a heated exchange of desire.

They were married two weeks later.

Looking back on that time Venetia concluded that for most of it she had been in a state of shock. She floated through the lengthening days with a frightening serenity, making decisions, working, coping with John's suspicions and insecurity.

It was as though, once the decision had been made, she was able to flow placidly along on a pre-ordained course, without fear, without misgivings, without any more agonising. She accepted that Ryan did not love her, but she knew that he would not jeopardise their marriage by falling in love with anyone else. Venetia was completely confident of her ability to satisfy him intellectually and physically. He would not need to go elsewhere for passion.

And he had had his love affair. With the tragedy of her death Elizabeth held his heart captive for ever. In that realm of the mind where she ruled she was eternally young and beautiful and loving, the standard against which he would always measure Venetia, and probably every other woman.

I will not let it hurt me, she vowed.

But as their wedding approached she found herself craving the reassurance their mutual desire gave her; at least there, in the sensual world they made for each other, there was no pretence. He had moved back into his flat, and although he saw her each day, he seemed quite contented to greet her with a soft brush of her lips which tantalised more than it satisfied. No impassioned embraces, none of the heated passion she craved; he was prepared to wait until after the ceremony.

The subsequent days proved that the breakthrough Ryan had achieved had been a permanent one. John no longer treated his father with suspicion or resentment, but relaxed into his usual sunny, inquisitive, confident self.

The night before the wedding Venetia sat with him out on the terrace and tried to explain what would be happening the next day.

'I know about weddings,' he told her importantly. 'I saw one on television. The lady had a long white dress on.'

She laughed and said, 'Well, I won't be wearing a long white dress.'

'OK, but afterwards me and you and Daddy are going to live at his place all together. And Pandy.'

They had decided that it would probably help John adjust better if there was no honeymoon. Venetia nodded.

He finished cheerfully, 'Daddy said he would buy me a train and sometimes he's going to play with it with me.'

It was clear that John was completely reconciled both to his new life and his father. Venetia gave him a sudden hug, holding him so tightly that he wriggled and pushed at her. He was growing up, she thought a little wistfully.

She had not expected to sleep very well that night, but her body took over and she lay like one dead, waking the next morning with a slight headache which vanished within a few minutes of the arrival of her uncle with a cup of tea. He was followed a little later by Janice, bearing a tray with breakfast daintily arranged on it.

'Traditional,' she said sternly when Venetia made a sound of protest. 'And eat it all up, otherwise you could feel faint. I remember I had to stand over Elizabeth——' She stopped precipitately, all the pleasure draining out of her face.

Venetia said softly, 'I know Liz married Ryan, it's silly to think that mentioning it will upset me.'

But Janice said as if she couldn't help herself, 'I still miss her.'

'I know.' Venetia put out a hand to pull her aunt down on the bed beside her.

She hugged the older woman's thin form while Janice wept. After a short time she blew her nose and straightened up. 'I'm sorry,' she said thickly. 'I wanted to make this such a happy day for you, and now I've spoiled it.'

'No, you haven't, of course we all remember Liz. We all mourn her.' Venetia covered her pain with a steady smile, patting her aunt's arm. 'Purely as a matter of interest, how have you managed to keep John quiet until now?'

Janice gave a choked laugh and said, 'Don't ask. A combination of bribery and threats and appeals to sweet reason. He's——'

As if he had heard his name he came running into the room and bounced up on to the bed, obviously in tearing good spirits with a smudge of what looked suspiciously like chocolate on his top lip. 'Hello, Mummy,' he said and gave her a smacking big kiss which almost over-turned the breakfast tray. 'Hurry up, it's time for the wedding!'

Even Janice laughed, and laughed more when John twinkled up at her and announced, 'I'm going to throw confetti all over Mummy and Daddy at the wedding. Mummy said I could.'

His tone left it in no doubt that this was going to be the high point of his day. Possibly even of his life up until then.

It was another glorious day, warm yet imbued with the freshhess that is spring's special gift. A beaming sun gilded the world and great white galleons of cloud moved majestically across a sky of glowing, gracious blue. As she dressed in the slim ivory dress she had chosen Venetia felt her heart expanding, becoming lighter and more buoyant.

On a day like this it was easy to believe that she and Ryan could have a happy marriage. It was even easy to believe that he might come to love her. She could no longer be jealous of Elizabeth's ghost. They had so much in common, she and Ryan, surely they could live together in mutual respect and affection, if that was all he could offer.

She would try, anyway. She would do her best to make him happy, ease the loneliness she suspected lay behind that very self-sufficient exterior, and give him the family life he was perhaps a little romantic about.

Venetia gave a last searching look in the mirror before turning away to get into her shoes; they were the same rich ivory as the silk dress. She pinned an exquisite gardenia to her tiny hat, adjusted the frivolous sweep of veiling to cover eyes which burned golden in her face and picked up gloves and bag, all the same colour as her dress. The outfit flattered her, far more sophisticated than the lace and tulle in pure virginal white that Elizabeth had worn; as she checked for the vital necessities carried in every woman's bag, Venetia said softly, 'I'll take care of him, Liz.'

In a way it was like saying goodbye, a farewell to the past and a promise for the future.

A knock on the door heralded her aunt, tentative and still a little shadowed about the eyes. 'May I come in?'

'Yes, of course, provided you haven't got John with you.'

Chuckling, Janice closed the door behind her. 'He and Bob are playing dominoes.' She looked Venetia over, her expression dazzled. 'You look lovely,' she said after a moment.

'Good.'

'Ryan will be very proud of you.' She sat carefully in the room's one chair and smiled a little wistfully. 'I must say, when I told Ryan about John I only hoped he'd bring you back to live here, but my subconscious must have been praying like mad for this to happen.'

Venetia had stopped spraying a light mist of perfume about her. In a voice she didn't recognise she said, 'So Ryan knew of John's existence before he arrived in Australia.'

'Yes,' Janice said. 'I thought he should know, and it didn't seem as though you were going to tell him.'

'I see.' She put the scent bottle down and checked the small gold studs in her ears. Why did it hurt so? It had been a foolish little illusion, that he had sought her out for herself. And like all illusions all it needed was the truth to shatter it. At least it explained Ryan's uncharacteristic calmness when confronted by the fact of his son's existence. He had had time to get over his first reaction, which had probably been murderous rage.

In a voice that was as clear and brittle as crystal Venetia said, 'Perhaps I should wear the cameos Gran left me. What do you think?'

'I like those little gold studs best,' her aunt replied with automatic honesty.

'I'm sure you're right. It must be time to go.'

The wedding was as quiet as they had planned for it to be, and John threw a whole box of confetti at them, laughing with such open glee at being encouraged to make a mess that any stiffness fled. Venetia found that she could not look at Ryan's tall, elegant figure, although she was aware that he was withdrawn, almost aloof.

Afterwards they all had lunch, complete with champagne, in a private room at one of Auckland's best restaurants. John stole a sip from Venetia's glass and decided that he liked it, although it wasn't as nice as lime juice, and then the three of them drove silently back to the flat.

'You, my brave warrior, had better have a rest,' Venetia told her son as he walked through the door, stifling his third yawn in five minutes.

He shuffled his feet, but only as a matter of form. 'OK. Daddy can tuck me in.'

Venetia watched them move down the passage to the room he had claimed for himself, then went into the main bedroom and took off her clothes, hanging them in the empty wardrobe which was now hers. Yesterday she and her aunt had brought all of her clothes and John's over and put them away, as well as the toys and books she had brought from Australia. Having familiar things about her should have helped to make her feel at home, but she had never felt so forlorn in her life.

She was standing in her plain cream slip when Ryan came in. He stopped just inside the door and watched her slight figure, alone and slightly drooping in the middle of the room. Eyes unfocused, she was staring out of the window, and she turned towards him with a visible effort.

'Don't look so apprehensive,' he said without any inflection at all in his deep voice.

Her smile was stiff on her face. 'Stupid, isn't it?'

'How long will he sleep?'

She hid her dilating eyes with her lashes. 'Half an hour, if we're lucky.'

He shrugged out of his jacket and the beautiful silk shirt he had on underneath it, tossing them both on the wide expanse of the bed. 'Not long enough,' he said quite calmly. 'Once I start making love to you I don't want to stop until I'm sated, and that could take all night. Are you planning to take root there? I'll make coffee while you check out the room I organised for your study. I've put what I've done on the script so far for you to look at.'

Laughter eased her dry mouth. She turned away from his dark, powerful presence, the wild restlessness in her body showing up only in the flickering movements of her lashes.

It was totally unfair that the mere sight of his bared torso could arouse her; she resented her weakness, yet the thought of never again feeling the swift, hot rush of desire through her nerves was frightening. Quickly, before he could see what his lean, tanned litheness was doing to her she turned away and without casting a glance his way changed into jeans and a cotton shirt and brushed her hair, letting it fall back into its neat, geometrical cut.

It's a workaday old world, she told herself, and smiled with irony. He was making it brutally clear that he expected nothing more than a companionable marriage enlivened by passion. And if she was going to be wounded each time he proved it she was going to end up numbed and shell-shocked, a basket case. So she called on every ounce of the hard, shining courage she used as armour and swung her hips in insouciant provocation as she preceded him out of the room.

Yesterday she and Janice had not had time to do any more than deposit inside the third bedroom the boxes containing her typewriter and a few reference books which she had bought in New Zealand. Someone, probably Ryan, had unpacked the books and put them on a shelf in a bookshelf beneath the window. On a wide console was a word processor, exactly the same model as the one she was used to, and a set of cupboards held office supplies. And on that there was a vase of flowers, deep prussian blue and gold Dutch irises which lent the somewhat cramped area a breath of spring.

'Is this the way you want it?' Ryan looked around, frowning slightly. 'You may prefer to be able to see out of the window.'

'No, I lose my concentration if there's anything to catch my attention. Thank you.'

'There's the script so far.'

She hadn't yet seen it and when she picked it up she was amazed at how much he had done. He must have driven himself during the last weeks, she thought, and wondered why. By now she knew just how busy he was, even with the help of the eager team he had attracted around him. Telephone calls from all around the world woke him at ungodly hours of the night, and always there seemed to be decisions which only he could make, work that only he could do.

Perhaps the long hours spent on the script had been attempts to stop himself from dwelling on the fact that he was going to be married to a woman he despised.

Six years ago she had used Albert Gamble's diaries for exactly that reason, to free her for a few hours from the grey misery which had enshrouded her; it would be ironically appropriate if her forebear was doing the same thing for Ryan!

A long time later she lifted weary, appreciative eyes from the sheets of paper. So far Ryan had made a superb job. He hadn't succumbed to the temptation to turn Albert into a southern hemisphere cowboy, all dash and daring, a flat figure with no depth. There was action aplenty in the diaries, but he had chosen those events from Albert's violent adventures which illuminated his complex character, carefully pointing up the dilemma of a man who had been torn between his lust for adventure and his compulsion to found a pastoral dynasty.

And Ryan had written with sensitivity and perception of the romance between the well-bred younger son of an upper-middle-class family stiff with Victorian conventions, and the girl of good reputation but no family who had come out to the colony to be a servant. In those days of extreme class-consciousness, even in New Zealand, such an alliance was viewed with suspicion and scorn; Ryan had dealt sympathetically with both sides of that passionate, turbulent romance.

John came wandering in, rosy-faced and thirsty. 'I want a drink, please,' he told her reproachfully. 'Daddy's talking on the phone.'

He was, speaking in a cryptic staccato which denoted trouble. When she had given John his drink she came back into the sitting-room and sent Ryan an enquiring look as he put the receiver down.

He said grimly, 'That was one of the bloodhounds of the Press.'

Her fine brows drew together. 'What did you tell them?'

He grinned, not very nicely. 'The bare facts. Now I'll start calling in a few favours. I have some clout; friends, contacts, people who owe me. I don't think we'll be bothered much by gossip columnists.'

John called out something from the kitchen and Ryan said tersely, 'If there are comments on the resemblance, look haughty and, if you can manage it, bewildered.'

She shrugged. 'If anyone comes straight out and remarks on it I'll just smile and agree.'

'It shouldn't be too bad.'

She believed him. Ryan was not a man to cross. He spent some time on the telephone and when he had finished switched on the answering machine. Then, as if the thought of reporters hungering for news gave him no qualms, he settled down to spend the rest of the afternoon helping John set out the train set they had chosen together.

After that he gave John his bath while Venetia discovered the meal the housekeeper had left prepared. As she did the few things necessary she heard Ryan's deep voice reading a story to his son. It was all very domesticated, as though the years between had been wiped away and they had always been like this, a family. It was too comforting a fantasy and she banished it; it made her too vulnerable.

After John had been tucked into bed they went back into the sitting-room. Venetia poured coffee as Ryan put a record on to the magnificent set and the lushly sensual strains of *Scheherezade* hid the sound of rain on the windows.

She felt as shy as the most virginal of Victorian brides, yet excited too, flushed and with eyes that gleamed like a cat's in the mellow light. Ryan sat down beside her on the sofa, disposing the muscled length of his legs with unconscious grace. She swallowed and handed him his coffee.

'You look nervous,' he said lazily, almost insolently.

She shrugged. 'Surprisingly enough, I am.'

He laughed and took her cup and put it down, then drew her into his arms.

What followed was what she had been waiting for, a relentless assault on her senses which began in gentleness and ended in a conflagration so intense that she found herself crying out in ecstasy, lost to everything but the violent release he extorted from her.

It was repeated, time after time in the weeks that followed, until she realised that for both of them there was not going to be the satiation he had promised himself. Each time they came together in the big bed it was with a hunger wondrously fresh and unappeased; they never tired of each other, found new delights, new ways of pleasuring each other and when it was over, locked together in the exhaustion of release, slept like two halves of a whole.

And they grew apart almost as fast as they relearned the secret language of sex. Within days Ryan's mood became savagely introverted; he worked long hours and seemed only to relax when he was with John. After an initial query which precipitated an icy withdrawal on his part, Venetia made no attempt to discover what was tearing at him.

She, too, retreated, sketching out a plan for her next novel, going Christmas shopping with John, taking him for walks in the park across the road—there was plenty to do even though the flat was efficiently cared for by Ryan's housekeeper. Venetia learned again the power of loneliness, but she tried to find satisfaction in the way John bloomed in his father's attention.

One night, arriving home most unusually late after John had gone to bed, Ryan said curtly, 'I had a call from the land agent today. He thinks he may have a house for us about twenty miles north, on the coast. I said we'd have a look at it tomorrow.'

Venetia turned over the card he had tossed at her. 'Very well,' she said. 'Have you had dinner?'

'Of a sort. I'm not hungry.'

He looked drained, tiredness emphasising harshly the aquiline features. Venetia suggested, 'Why don't you have a shower and go to bed? I'll bring you a drink.'

He laughed shortly and bent to kiss her hard. 'If I go to bed, I won't want a drink,' he said with calculated mockery. 'As you know. Why don't you just ask me to make love to you?'

'I wasn't aware that I needed to ask,' she retorted crisply. 'I make love to you too, or hadn't you noticed?'

'Oh, I've noticed. I think I'll go down into hell remembering what it was like to have you love me. All that fire and sweet, dangerous lust . . . That's all I'll have to remember, because that's all you feel, isn't it?'

The telephone was an opportune interruption, stopping the smoothly vicious comments which penetrated like poisoned arrows all the way to her heart. As he snatched up the receiver she turned to go out of the room but stopped with clenched stomach when she heard him say in the silky voice of ultimate rage, 'Yes, my wife is here. Wait a moment, please.'

He was smiling, but she shuddered as she took the receiver, her eyes enormous in her face. Still in that terrifying voice he said, 'He didn't give his name, but it's your ex-husband. Get rid of him.'

'Sean?' she croaked.

'Hi, love of my life.' He sounded bright and very pleased with himself. 'Listen, sorry to bother you but I've just had dinner with cousin Brett, and during it he divulged what he's been doing with the shares my daft Aunt Gabby gave us for a wedding present, God rest her soul. I gave them to him to do what he liked with as soon as we got them, remember? And, as my cousin Brett is a wizard at the financial wheeling and dealing, they've turned into quite a nice little nest-egg.'

She was bewildered, her eyes locked on to the menacing darkness of Ryan's. 'I'm sorry, I don't understand.'

'Well, they are half yours, you know.'

'No!' she exclaimed vehemently. 'No, Sean, I couldn't!'

With the stubbornness she remembered well, he insisted, 'But they were a wedding present, therefore you are entitled to——'

'Oh no, no, I don't want——'

She could hear him protesting away as the receiver was jerked from her hand. Into it Ryan said in a molten voice, 'My wife does not want anything from you, March, and I don't want you contacting her again.' He hung up and demanded through his teeth, 'Have you been seeing him?'

Appalled, she said, 'No, I have not.' She told him what Sean had called for, and some of the black fury in his expression dissipated.

'I'm glad you didn't want the money,' he said brusquely as she turned away, 'because your tyrant of a husband would have forbidden you to accept it. I've had enough of Sean Bloody March to last me a lifetime.'

'Oh, so *you* have had enough!' She whirled back to face him, her eyes a clear, blazing gold in her drawn face. 'I have had it to *here* with you and your bloody moods, one minute pulling me towards you, the next pushing me away as though my touch contaminated you! All you want from me is sex, and you make me pay for that fact, because you hate yourself for it, don't you? It demeans you in your own eyes to want a woman as much as you want me! How the hell did you treat Elizabeth, or didn't you want her?'

His head jolted back as though she had struck him, but his mouth was taut and cruel, the white line around it revealing the tight rein he held on his temper. Through clenched teeth he said, 'We'll leave Elizabeth out of this.'

'How can we?' Overwrought, she struck her small fist against the door-frame, uncaring of the pain because it helped to mask the more dreadful agony which was clawing at her. 'She's the third member of this—this farce we call a marriage, she's with us all day, every night. Even when you have to pander to the base instincts you so de-

spise and make love to me! You start off making love to
Elizabeth, sweetly, tenderly, and then you realise it's the
wrong woman and you turn into another man, intent on
making me suffer because I'm not her!' She drew a deep,
sobbing breath, cradling her maltreated hand unconsciously as she finished in a voice torn by feeling, 'Did
you really think that I wouldn't know?'

He was pale, the strong features rigid with some intolerable emotion. Without speaking he came towards her
small, stiff figure and took her hand, examining it carefully. After a moment his dark, impenetrable gaze moved
back to her anguished face. He blinked, as though he was
exhausted. 'Come and sit down,' he commanded tonelessly.

He was going to admit it, she knew it, and to have her
convictions confirmed was going to kill her, but she made
no demur. Better the truth, however painful, than the lies
and evasions with which they had cloaked their motives
for so long. At least with the truth there was some possibility of building anew.

Like a small ghost she allowed him to put her into a
chair and watched with a dead, bruised look to her face
as he sat on the sofa opposite. He didn't look at her as he
began to speak.

'I change when we're making love because there is
nothing else I can do. When I touch you I want nothing
else, I lose myself in you...' He pushed his fingers
wretchedly through his hair, then continued, 'Elizabeth
was kind and serene and gentle. And she loved me, she
thought that I was everything her husband should be. She
didn't understand me, but that didn't worry her, because everyone knows that men are strange kittle-cattle,
they operate on a different plane. She really thought like
that. She was warm and feminine, and all that she asked
of me was that I fit into her conception of a husband. It
isn't fair to say that she was shallow, because she felt
deeply, but for her love was a gentle, calm emotion. I

don't know how long we had been married when I realised what sort of mistake I had made. Only a matter of months.'

He paused for so long that she thought he couldn't finish. In a voice that was totally empty of feeling Venetia said, 'Go on.'

'She didn't know that there are depths—great chasms—and heights, soaring, perfect ecstatic heights to love. She could never have understood that you can both love and hate someone at the same time. She thought that sort of intense, uncontrolled emotion a little vulgar, somewhat pretentious. She didn't really believe that it exists, because she was incapable of feeling it. Or perhaps because she never met the man who could rouse it in her.'

Outside the rain spattered against the windows; a dreary little wind began to mourn around the eaves. Venetia sat very still, surprised to discover that she was breathing, that her heart was beating through the quiet avenues of her body.

He looked up. She could see nothing beyond the polite façade of his expression. In a toneless voice he said, 'The kind of passion you exact from me, the stupendous, total submersion in each other—Elizabeth wouldn't have wanted, nor understood that. I discovered that I wanted both of you.'

Harshly, because her disappointment was almost equalled by her anger, she said, 'Me for sex, her for love.'

'No. You for my wife, her as a friend.'

'But you didn't love me,' she whispered.

He gave her a sombre, almost angry glance, his mouth twisted and hard. 'I didn't know you, did I? You took good care that no one saw through the assertive, brittle, amusing persona you presented to the world. You protected yourself by hiding your real character so successfully that everyone was completely hoodwinked. As I was.'

She couldn't speak but he nodded and said, 'Yes. And your behaviour was calculated to reinforce that tough, aggressive image. I was amused by your nerve and stimulated by your intelligence. As a lover you couldn't be faulted, eager, uninhibited, a sensuous, ardent little wildcat in bed. There has never been another woman who could make me feel the way you do.'

'You resented that. You still do.'

He nodded, his heavy lids falling to hide his eyes. 'Oh yes. I was afraid. I had learned that it was dangerous to want love, dangerous to give it. It was vital for me to remain in control of my emotions.'

Painfully, because more than anything she wanted to believe him and it was difficult, she objected, 'But I saw you fall in love with Elizabeth. I was there, I watched it happen.'

'You saw me meet a pretty, gentle girl who appeared to combine the best characteristics of my mistress and the sort of wife I thought I wanted.' He saw her wince but went on bluntly, 'I was vulnerable to that. My childhood had predisposed me to demand that the woman I chose for a wife be prepared to give up everything, not so much for me but for our children. You had made it quite clear that you had no intention of doing that, so Elizabeth was—a compromise, if you like. I convinced myself that she was a magical combination of your sensuality and the gentleness you didn't possess. It's humiliating for me to accept that I'm just as capable as anyone else of hiding from the truth behind a mask of evasions and wishful thinking and rationalisations.'

He shrugged as though his lack of insight was a weight, a burden he hated, before continuing, 'So I sought Elizabeth out and she seemed to be all that I needed. Then you came back from your trip to the Islands and you pushed me beyond my limits again so that I lost control and took you in a way which has always haunted me.'

She couldn't bear the self-contempt she saw in his face but she could only say stupidly, 'It doesn't matter.'

'Of course it matters,' he said tiredly, condemning himself far more harshly than she ever could. 'It was barbaric.'

Venetia astounded herself by giving a small smile. 'I think there's something barbaric about the way we feel,' she said softly.

He nodded, answering with a wry twist of his lips. 'Yes. It's not fair to discuss Elizabeth any further, but believe this, if you believe nothing else. When we make love I don't—I can't—think of anyone else but you, and what you do to me, and how to make sure that you are receiving the same ecstasy you give me. You are as much woman as I can handle.'

'Was Elizabeth happy?'

His surprise was quickly replaced by thought. After a moment he said slowly, 'Yes, she was happy. She had what she wanted; she thought that I was as fulfilled as she was. She never knew that I was in love with you.'

Her response to that was a long, sighing breath with a question on it. 'How do you know that?'

'Because,' he admitted, his features chiselled into bleakness, 'I didn't know myself. I didn't know until I realised in Australia, the night I saw you comforting John after his nightmare, that if you wouldn't marry me I'd be alone and lonely for the rest of my life. I told you, remember, that I'd confused Elizabeth with you and that it wasn't going to happen again. That night I realised that I'd been in love with you all along, and that I'd condemned us both to years of loneliness because I was a coward. I was afraid to love. My experience with my mother had taught me that loving exposes you to pain and rejection and a humiliating dependence. I married Elizabeth because I knew that she'd never reject me—and because she wanted nothing from me but affection. You demanded everything.'

She opened her mouth to speak, but he went on in a goaded voice, 'If I needed any reinforcement it came when you danced with Sean March and I was seared by jealousy so intense that it hurt to breathe.'

She stared at him as if he were crazy. 'You came to Australia for John. Janice said that she told you about him.'

'Yes, she did, and he was the excuse. Oh, I wanted him, but he was just an abstract figure, a boy, not John Ryan Fraine. I had to learn to love him. But you——'

He put out a hand and pulled her on to the sofa, holding her still as he swung his long legs up and stretched out beside her. His expression was enigmatic, but she could see the glow deep in his eyes and felt her own body clench in helpless, conditioned response.

'You,' he repeated, his voice heavy and hard, shaking with emotion he no longer troubled to hide, 'I took one look at you and knew that that was it, I'd spent the last six years with hunger for you eating at my heart.'

He brought his head down to rest on the tender haven of her breast. His face was very warm, almost feverish, and she could feel the rapid thumping of his heart against her skin. 'I starved for you,' he muttered, turning his head so that the roughness of his stubble acted as a delicious friction through the material of her dress. 'I couldn't sleep at night, I used to wake dreaming of you and reach for you and find that it was Elizabeth, so sweet, so charming, so patently lacking in anything but affection and a mild pleasure in my embraces. She thought our love life was eminently satisfactory, she used to tell me what a wonderful lover I was, and she really believed it to be true, but I could remember your wild eyes and laughing, biting mouth and the strange little sounds you used to make in your throat when we made love, and I knew that I had—that I had thrown away the pearl of great price for a pretty imitation in mother-of-pearl. And I could never leave her, never have you, because she would never have understood, it would have killed her. I found then what it is like to be alone. I thought I was going to have to spend the rest of my life like that. But it wasn't until I saw you with our son in your arms that I realised what I felt for you was love.'

She shivered. 'Do you feel guilty because she died?'

'No.' He lifted his head from his ardent exploration of the curve beneath her breast, and met her eyes, his for once completely open, all barriers fallen. 'No, I'm even glad now that she had those years with me, because she was happy, Venetia. The only thing that marred her happiness was a feeling of guilt about you, but she had no conception of the hell you must have gone through.'

He looked at her straight, demanding an answer. Her arms looped about his neck, pulling his head down until his mouth was a whisper away from hers. 'Of course I loved you,' she said softly. 'I think I loved you the first time I saw you. I love you now. When I'm dying I'll call for you and if you're not in paradise when I get there I'll follow you down into hell!'

He laughed and got up, pulling her with him, and carried her down the hall and into the bedroom and put her gently, lovingly, on to the bed. His face was irradiated by an emotion she had never seen there before; he sat on the bed beside her and smiled down at her and she felt the same emotion glow through the fleshy covering of her features, and knew that for her as for him, from now on, this happiness would last as long as they did.

He leaned down and kissed her with aching tenderness, then with the throbbing sensuality she needed so much. Against her mouth he whispered, 'We go together, you and I, two halves of the one whole. And if you have to follow me down to hell, hell will become all the paradise I want . . .'

Two lives, two destinies

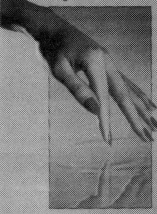

–but the same fate?

Cynthia Warner discovers frightening similarities between her own life and that of Karla Hoffman. Even down to the same marriage difficulties they experience.

The one alarming exception is that Karla was murdered in Cynthia's house 50 years before.

Is Cynthia destined to suffer the same fate?

An enthralling novel by Andrew Neiderman

Available December 1987 Price £2.95

W✪RLDWIDE

YOU'RE INVITED TO ACCEPT **FOUR ROMANCES** AND A TOTE BAG

FREE!

Acceptance card

| NO STAMP NEEDED | Post to: **Reader Service, FREEPOST, P.O. Box 236, Croydon, Surrey. CR9 9EL** |

Please note readers in Southern Africa write to:
Independant Book Services P.T.Y., Postbag X3010, Randburg 2125, S. Africa

YES! Please send me 4 free Mills & Boon Romances and my free tote bag – and reserve a Reader Service Subscription for me. If I decide to subscribe I shall receive 6 new Romances every month as soon as they come off the presses for £7.20 together with a FREE monthly newsletter including information on top authors and special offers, exclusively for Reader Service subscribers. There are no postage and packing charges, and I understand I may cancel or suspend my subscription at any time. If I decide not to subscribe I shall write to you within 10 days. Even if I decide not to subscribe the 4 free novels and the tote bag are mine to keep forever. I am over 18 years of age   EP20R

NAME _____
                                        (CAPITALS PLEASE)

ADDRESS _____

_____

_____ POSTCODE _____

The right is reserved to refuse application and change the terms of this offer. You may be mailed with other offers as a result of this application. Offer expires March 31st 1988 and is limited to one per household.
Offer applies in UK and Eire only. Overseas send for details.

ROMANCE

Variety is the spice of romance

Each month Mills & Boon publish new romances. New stories about people falling in love. A world of variety in romance – from the best writers in the romantic world. Choose from these titles in December.

AN AWAKENING DESIRE Helen Bianchin
SMOKE IN THE WIND Robyn Donald
MAN OF IRON Catherine George
RELUCTANT PRISONER Stephanie Howard
STORM CLOUD MARRIAGE Roberta Leigh
WISH FOR THE MOON Carole Mortimer
HARMONIES Rowan Kirby
LIVING DANGEROUSLY Elizabeth Oldfield
THE ORTIGA MARRIAGE Patricia Wilson
WICKED INVADER Sara Wood
*A THOUSAND ROSES Bethany Campbell
*A PAINFUL LOVING Margaret Mayo
*THE GAME IS LOVE Jeanne Allan
*CLOUDED PARADISE Rachel Ford

On sale where you buy paperbacks. If you require further information or have any difficulty obtaining them, write to: Mills & Boon Reader Service, PO Box 236, Thornton Road, Croydon, Surrey CR9 3RU, England.

*These four titles are available from Mills & Boon Reader Service.

Mills & Boon
the rose of romance

 **ROMANCE**

Next month's romances from Mills & Boon

Each month, you can choose from a world of variety in romance with Mills & Boon. These are the new titles to look out for next month.

FORECAST OF LOVE Katherine Arthur
WITCH'S HARVEST Sara Craven
WHIRLPOOL OF PASSION Emma Darcy
JENNY'S TURN Vanessa Grant
FIGHT FOR LOVE Penny Jordan
FRAZER'S LAW Madeleine Ker
WHEN LOVERS MEET Flora Kidd
REASONS OF THE HEART Susan Napier
DISHONOURABLE INTENTIONS Sally Wentworth
BID FOR INDEPENDENCE Yvonne Whittal
* **NO PLACE TO RUN** Jane Donnelly
* **CAPTURE A NIGHTINGALE** Sue Peters
* **A STAR FOR A RING** Kay Gregory
* **NO LOVE IN RETURN** Avery Thorne

Buy them from your usual paperback stockist, or write to: Mills & Boon Reader Service, P.O. Box 236, Thornton Rd, Croydon, Surrey CR9 3RU, England. Readers in Southern Africa — write to: Independent Book Services Pty, Postbag X3010, Randburg, 2125, S. Africa.

*These four titles are available from Mills & Boon Reader Service.

Mills & Boon
the rose of romance

Unwrap Temptation This Christmas.

As the first Temptation pack produced last year proved such a success
with our readers, we have decided to publish a second.
It consists of three irresistibly sensual romances aimed at today's woman:

MYSTERY TRAIN	**Lynn Turner**
RISKY PLEASURE	**Jo Ann Ross**
THE WAITING GAME	**Jayne Ann Krentz.**

Succumb to Temptation this Christmas with Mills and Boon.

Available November 1987 Price: £3.60

Available from Boots, Martins, John Menzies, W H Smith,
Woolworths and other paperback stockists.